A UNICORN'S GUIDE TO THE MULTIVERSE

Daniel McCaslin

Copyright © 2023 by Minor Flock Publishing, LLC

All rights reserved. No part of this book may be reproduced or used in any manner without written permission of the copyright owner except for the use of quotations in a book review. For more information, address:

info@minorflock.com

Minor Flock Publishing, LLC

1501 N Charlotte Ave Suite A104

Monroe, NC 28110

First paperback edition May 2023

Book design by Casey Fritz, Albatross Book Co.

9798395291714 (paperback)

ISBN 978-8-89034-314-7 (ebook)

www.minorflock.com

One

THERE'S NO BRIGHT RED exit sign for people to follow when they want to leave life behind - no clear path to follow when the world around you seems to be burning down. If it were that distinct and present, more people may choose to follow it before their time to leave came.

Charlie eschewed the norm of wandering through life while waiting for the unexpected to happen. If no clear exit sign was going to present itself, he was intent on creating his own.

Stepping out of his dilapidated car, he looked back at the rust-red coloring that covered the two-door sedan he had owned since he was a teenager, avoiding the reflection looking back at him from the windshield. It had been the first big purchase he had made, and it was the escape hatch he used to part ways with the life he was tethered to at his childhood home. It had broken down more times than he could count but it never seemed appropriate to leave it to die peacefully in a junk yard.

He wondered for a moment what would happen to

it when people realized it was his, and its owner was no longer in need of its service. He had no friends to leave it to, and he doubted his family would want it around.

Turning from his car, Charlie faced the trailhead that would lead him up the mountain. The world had continuously disappointed him, so why would today be any different? An early snowstorm had left the ground covered in a fine white coating of winter. Snowfall can have an infectious beauty, but it was now an obnoxious distraction to the plan he had etched out a month before his arrival.

If it fell too heavy in the valley beneath the peak...

He didn't let himself continue the thought.

"I didn't come here to be turned away," he muttered to himself.

He feared turning 30. He didn't know why or what would be so disheartening by reaching the apparent milestone, but he was intent on not letting it happen. He had few hours left before midnight and he wanted to reach the bottom of the mountain before the next day could reach him.

Trudging up the trail, Charlie continued muttering to himself, ignoring the odd looks he received from passersby who were making their way down from the peak. He had chosen a sunset hike so that he would be alone and unbothered at the peak. Night-fall would take hold of the mountain before he arrived at the rocky outcropping he had loved since his first visit to the grand view it offered.

It was only when he was in the mountains that Charlie ever felt at ease; something he had longed for in his time whenever he was around people, including members of his own family. The youngest of four, he'd never felt the connection so many of the kids he grew up with shared with their families. As he had grown older, he let distance do the work of finding ways to be more isolated from their reach.

His trek to the peak was uneventful, and as the sun set, the somber mood of the wooded trail put him at ease. The songbirds were asleep, but the music of nature still played in the rustling of the pine trees in the wind as he found his way to the rocky outcropping at the end of the trail.

Sitting alone on the peak, Charlie stared at the stars in the vast, clear sky. The Milky Way's swirling arm was glowing faintly overhead. He pulled out a sandwich he had packed to ease into his final moments. He wanted a reason to sit and think – a reason to let certainty conquer his doubts.

Charlie ate half of his sandwich and took a swig of water from the canteen he'd had with him on every hike for the last ten years. Covered in stickers, dents, and memories, it felt like an old friend. He spent the next moments convincing himself he had enjoyed enough rich experiences that this would be a proper one to end on.

Too full to eat anymore, he took a few puffs of his vape. If his stomach was too bloated, it might mess up his jump, and he needed everything to go right. He tossed the remaining half of the sandwich down the trail so a hungry animal might enjoy it. Pulling his bag to his feet, Charlie opened the zipper and pulled out a single sheet of paper he had tucked securely in its confines. He read over the words that he had spent the last few weeks editing. It was uncomfortable to read.

The intent of the words typed out had always been in the future. Faced with the finality of their purpose, Charlie had to fight past the urge to wait and give himself more time. He placed the note back in his bag, making sure to not crumple the paper to avoid the distortion of the words.

Convinced his bag was secure, Charlie began to remove his boots. They were still in good shape with a healthy tread ready for many more miles. In his note, he asked that they be given to a local outdoors shop he frequented. He saw no need to waste a perfectly good pair of boots.

His toes immediately felt the chill, and the snow started to soak through his socks. The cold made his mind feel exquisitely alert. He walked to the edge of the cliff in his socks.

"Here's to nothingness," he said. One last drag from his vape was all he needed. He looked at the stars and said goodbye.

He took his final steps without hesitation. One foot swung over the abyss, and the other foot started to follow, and he closed his eyes on existence.

He didn't feel the air rushing to meet him. He didn't hear the wind screaming in his ears. He didn't feel weightless or dizzy or nauseated. He felt absolutely nothing because absolutely nothing had happened. His body remained stuck in place on the peak.

Opening his eyes, Charlie saw the vast expanse he was supposed to have plunged into. But he was still on the mountain. It made no sense. He felt something tugging on the back of his shirt, and he turned around angrily, ready to punish whoever felt important enough to sabotage his meticulous plan.

"What the fuck?" The unexplainable appearance at his feet fought to pull him backward. Charlie stared into its scribbled-on eyes, unable to process what life had created to stop him from reaching the exit sign he installed in the valley below.

Two

"Seriously, you need to stop this," the unicorn said. It had a cardboard jaw on which misshapen teeth had been drawn. Its crooked horn was made from an old toilet paper roll. Charlie tried to touch it, but the unicorn backed away, yanking Charlie's body to a safe and secure spot atop the peak.

"How do I know you're real if I can't touch you?" Charlie asked. Frustration and curiosity were merging in his mind as he contemplated the depths of insanity that could have summoned the visitor before him.

"We've been over this before, Charlie. I'm me. One of one. A completed version of an existent matter. You, on the other hand, are a tiny fraction of an infinite scroll, too incapable of even seeing down the page to catch a glimpse of the rest of yourselves."

Charlie's hand was still reaching for the unicorn. He wasn't ready to give up on death but his mind was waking to the reality he still inhabited.

"Fine," it said, inching forward. "You can touch me,

but just know you're going to regret it since I haven't been able to inoculate you."

As soon as Charlie's finger made contact with the crooked horn, he crumbled to the snowy ground and began convulsing. His mind scattered to distant realms, and he witnessed fleeting visions of alternate versions of his life as if he were scrolling through TV channels hoping for something to grab his attention.

"Just know you've earned this pain from idiocy and a lack of being able to listen," the unicorn said, pacing around Charlie and prodding his head with its front hooves. "You're going to make me do the thing, aren't you?"

The unicorn jumped onto Charlie's stomach and shoved its muzzle into Charlie's mouth, prying it wide enough until its entire head and horn fit inside. "Initiate bypass!" the unicorn shouted.

Charlie suddenly gagged and pushed the unicorn off, his jaw collapsing to its normal size. The unexpected expansion of his body had left him with a pounding headache, but the uncontrollable surge of visions in his mind finally ceased.

"Why?" Charlie shouted as he backed away. He could feel the cold snow seeping through his clothes, the biting chill penetrating his body and bones. "Why did you do that?"

"I didn't do anything but reverse your bad decision, twice."

Charlie stared into the unicorn's pink eyes, which

were scribbled on its face as if a child had drawn them.

"All I did was touch you and you broke me!" Charlie exclaimed.

"All I did was tell you to stop, and you and your finite intelligence refused to listen. Maybe next time, you act like someone with a firm grasp of auditory receptiveness and take an un-cosmically bound being at its word," the unicorn replied.

"What?" Charlie muttered, his expression blank.

"Great," the unicorn said. "Another bottom of the barrel version." The unicorn prodded Charlie's ear with one hoof. "Listen. Listen. It's always important to listen."

Charlie's head nodded up and down, but it was getting hard for him to tell if he was doing so out of compliance, or if he was entering the first stages of hypothermia. Using his last few ounces of bodily control, Charlie grabbed a handful of snow and smacked the unicorn's snout with it.

"Don't be a dick," he said.

"Why is your type so infatuated with anger and violence?"

"Why are you breaking my mind?" Charlie shouted as he considered having lost his mental faculties.

His voice scattered the wildlife that had gathered around the remnants of the sandwich, their squeals and hurried movements filling the silence that had formed between Charlie and the unicorn.

The unicorn lowered its head and scratched its brow

with a hoof. "Let's restart this scenario. You can call me Frids."

"That's a weird name. You have a weird name."

"It's not a name, it's an acronym better suited for you to understand."

Scooting forward, the unicorn brushed against Charlie's knee before settling its hind end in the snow. Charlie shivered. He'd always tried to avoid touching people he didn't know very well. He backed away and his hand slipped over the edge of the cliff. He remembered why he was at the peak. He still had time to carry through with it before the early morning hikers arrived.

"If it's an acronym, what does it stand for?"

"Frequency Radiating in Interdimensional Space."

"Cool." Growing weary of the situation, Charlie peered over the cliff. "Nice to meet you, Frids, but I have a reservation for one at the bottom of this mountain, and I don't want to be late."

"That's an unpleasant goodbye," the unicorn said, "but just know I've done the calculations, and your chances of actually dying have dropped considerably with the snowfall. The more likely outcome is that you'll just break your back, your legs, multiple ribs, and receive a serious skull fracture. None of which will kill you instantly." The unicorn's sides shook as it peered over the edge to verify its conclusion. "But it will leave you in sheer agony for hours until you succumb to your injuries or until another hiker spots you and calls a rescue team. The chances of you surviving are enough that if you recover, you will be forced to try and kill yourself again in a much less grandiose manner. And that's if you're even able to try and kill yourself again considering you may become paraplegic from the injuries. Plus, you'll have to spend a lot of time around your family and doctors in the hospital, and they will shame you for what you did." The unicorn seemed pleased with himself, satisfied with the undisputable evidence it was presenting. "Not an ideal situation in my opinion, but I'm sure you'll find a way to be happy with that outcome."

Charlie peered into the dark landscape below the cliff, searching the shadows for a spot that wasn't covered with thick, soft snow so that he could prove the unicorn wrong. When he turned around, Frids was next to him again, its mouth slightly open and his rear end shaking like a happy puppy waiting to be acknowledged.

"You're still a dick."

"It's fun to bond with new friends."

"We're not friends. I may be suicidal but I'm not crazy enough to think a hallucination is real."

Rather than wait for a response from his frustrating companion, Charlie walked past the unicorn and retrieved his backpack. Pulling the headlamp out of the front pocket, he clicked it on, the light bouncing across the white snow. He swung the pack to his back and secured the straps around his waist as he searched for the entrance to the trail, catching sight of a squirrel nibbling on the tasty brioche he had bought just for this night. Even his last meal was a failure. He let out a deep sigh and began walking.

"Everybody needs a friend, Charlie," Frids called out behind him.

"Friends are just people you acquire to attend your funeral."

"From the information I've attained, I think there are a few more things between the act of making a friend and dying."

"Nothing of consequence," Charlie said, his mood growing sour, unpleased as the conversation was gravitating toward a lecture on why the world is a happy place. "Friends are fine for people who need the reassurance that they matter and the bad advice that comes along with it."

"Nihilism and apathy don't make good bedfellows, Charlie. And what if you found a friend that could offer something of great consequence?"

"Highly unlikely, but thank you for wasting my night." Charlie grabbed his vape from his pocket and began taking long drags, letting the vapor fill the cold air in front of him.

Frids trotted ahead then stopped, blocking Charlie's progress. "Charlie, if you commit suicide, you may be taking the entire multiverse to its grave with you."

Staring dumbfounded at the unicorn, Charlie focused on the bent horn so as to avoid the scribbled smile and eyes.

"What?"

"How's that for a consequence?"

"Why would me committing suicide have any impact or relevance to the multiverse, if it even exists?"

"It does exist," Frids responded, standing up on his hindlegs and pushing Charlie to sit on a large rock. "And sure, if one of you killed themselves, it would be of no consequence whatsoever. Even if a million of you did it, same thing. No consequence. But if every version throughout the infinite realities that permeate the multiverse do it, big problem."

"Huh?"

"Right. You're a bottom-of-the-barrel version."

"Not appreciating the insults to my intelligence."

"More of an insult to your genetic structure than it is to you as a sentient and unintelligent being, but point taken."

When Frids took a seat in front of Charlie, he became cautiously optimistic that he could kick the unicorn aside and walk away in peace. But the fear of reliving the visions that ensued from his last encounter with the cardboard exterior of his unwelcome visitor made him rethink his plan. Shaking his head, he took a seat beside the unicorn as he readied himself for the journey back down the trail.

"Think of your infinite selves as a single chess piece in the multiverse. A pawn to be precise. I'd say a King or a Queen, but I think it's more relevant to stick to analogies that fit your accepted role in life."

"Fuck you, too."

"You're welcome. Now, as that pawn, even if you broke off a piece of it, you would still be able to use it in the game. You could break off a nice big chunk of it, and the piece would still be recognizable and useable. But if you were to take away the entire piece, the board would become unbalanced and the entire game would collapse. The board must be balanced. Understand?"

"Not at all."

"Charlie," Frids said, the unicorn's voice losing its cheerful tone and becoming exasperated. "Every version of you throughout the entire multiverse is killing themselves. If all of you disappear, then the entire universe collapses into a paradox from not being able to continue playing the game."

"Wait. Chess pieces are lost during the game of play. That's how the game is played. So no thank you." Charlie got up and headed down the trail. "The game will carry on just fine without me."

"Chess pieces may be lost, but they're kept by the side of the board to be used again in the same game, or a new game. Your infinite versions killing themselves removes the piece from ever being used again. When you kill yourself, your matter dissipates from its universe, traversing to my interdimensional plane, and can no longer be used. You deciding to not kill yourself is the key factor to letting the multiverse continue playing the game."

"That's nice," Charlie said. "But analogies aside, I'm

still going to kill myself. Bodies decay naturally, and the remains are absorbed by other forms of life. I'm leaving to go home now and would like you to return to whatever version of reality you belong in."

The annoying voice of Frids followed Charlie as he went down the mountain. The night was turning into a complete bust.

"Charlie!" Frids shouted commandingly. "At least let me give you a glimpse of the multiverse you'll be condemning along with yourself. Let me show you why your committing suicide will be the unraveling thread that tears all of existence apart. What's the harm in that?"

"Besides the fact you're most likely a hallucination?" Charlie responded. "I need to get home before my family checks up on me, which they regularly do since my former failed suicide attempt. If they see me talking to an imaginary unicorn, they will lock me up in a mental institution where I'll be put under 24-hour surveillance."

"What makes you think other people can't see me?" the unicorn said.

Charlie hurried down the trail, brushing aside branches and stumbling on rocks and fallen limbs. Part of the reason he was up here was because he felt his family cared so little about him. They didn't want to talk about his suicidal impulses, but when it came up, they always told him the same thing: "Just think about what you're leaving behind."

Thinking about what he'd be leaving behind was exactly why he wanted to jump off a mountain peak.

"If there is an infinite number of me in the multiverse, then can't you just count me as a loss and go find one who might be more receptive to your annoying request?"

"I like you the best, though."

Charlie stopped and stared at Frids.

"You've tried several before me, haven't you?" he said slowly.

"Dozens. But that doesn't take away from me wanting to keep you alive." Frids shook his head. "We're losing time now. As other Charlies continue to kill themselves, the growth rate of matter lost increases exponentially across the multiverse leading to an ever-evaporating timeline for me to solve the puzzle."

"This doesn't make sense! How can me dying of old age versus me dying of suicide have any effect on what the matter I'm made of does? How could it possibly know the difference?"

"The culmination of all your lives ending in suicide shows that it does, and I need to halt its progress."

Tired of trying to deal with Frids's puzzling claims, Charlie closed his eyes and leaned his head back, breathing in the cold air. When he opened his eyes, he could see the faint glow of the sun waking in the sky.

"Fine."

"Wait, that worked?"

"For now." Charlie shoved past the unicorn again

and picked up his pace. "I want coffee and quiet, though. Leave me alone and let me wrap my head around this."

"Can do. Absolutely. I just need to stick as close as possible to you to make sure you don't kill yourself."

"That would be the opposite of leaving me alone, and I highly doubt you'd be able to shut your mouth long enough for me to have more than a few moments of quiet. Not to mention that if people can actually see you, they're all going to demand to speak to the fantastical cardboard unicorn!"

"If you didn't want to mention it, then why did you?"

"Can you just shut up for a few hours?"

"I love quiet. I spent most of my existence in silence. I'm just trying out your vernacular so that I can properly communicate with the different versions of you."

"Point taken!" Charlie's anger was growing brighter by the minute. The early hikers hoping to beat the crowds would be on the trails soon. "Now can you disappear so I don't get locked in a mental institution or, worse, become the next sought-after guest for the most inane morning shows on earth?"

"Yes. Just one question. What's a morning show?"

"Fuck!" Charlie's shout rang through the trees, rousing the sleeping birds and scattering them throughout the canopy.

Charlie reached his breaking point. He swiftly swung his leg, trying to kick Frids in the head, throwing caution to the wind. Darting in and out of sight, Frids avoided the kick and Charlie's foot collided with a moss-covered log. He screamed with pain and farther down the trail a voice shouted, "Everything alright?"

The early hikers had arrived. Charlie looked around for Frids but the unicorn had disappeared. He briefly imagined that he had finally rid himself of the unwanted hallucination.

"Yeah, I'm good", he called out. "Just kicked a rock for the hundredth time." He didn't want anyone running up to rescue him.

"Been there," the hiker called out.

"That was a close one," Frids whispered in Charlie's ear.

Charlie swung around and smacked his cheek against the unicorn's horn. Frids was tucked inside his backpack, flashing that ever-present smile. He braced himself for a surge of horrible visions, but nothing happened.

"If you want me to not kill myself, please give me some peace by shutting up and disappearing for a while."

"I'll give you your peace and quiet. Just know I'll be watching."

Frids dropped farther inside Charlie's backpack, the zipper closing before Charlie could stop it. It was unnerving not to know how the unicorn had slipped in there without him realizing and without adding an ounce of extra weight.

"Why is death so hard?" he muttered, hurrying on-ward to his car.

Three

Driving back to town, Charlie was barely able to keep his eyes focused on the road. A mixture of exhaustion and overstimulation was pushing him to the point of delirium. To counteract it, he slid into his morning routine, parking the car in the garage under his apartment building and walking straight to his favorite coffee shop. Having little desire for a career, he had even taken a job there. Serving coffee and fresh meals would never lead to a life of luxury, but it had kept him close to a small semblance of happiness.

He was tempted to leave his backpack in the car, but he wanted to stick to the comfort of his usual routine, and his usual routine included his backpack at his side.

As Charlie sat at the counter waiting for his coffee and bagel, he looked around. People were messy, and even in his off hours he couldn't surpass the urge to clean up their sloppy intrusions on his life. Napkins were left behind and crumbs were scattered about, and Charlie succumbed to the urge to clean them up before his order arrived. He reached into the front pocket of his backpack, avoiding the larger pocket that Frids had disappeared into, and sifted through the few belongings he'd carried to his would-be end. He pulled out his phone and its charger. He'd let the battery die the day before, assuming he had no more need of it.

Charlie plugged the phone into an outlet on the wall beside him, then grabbed a wet wipe from his bag so he could clean the counter. He was trying to avoid the deafening silence of zero notifications of people trying to contact him.

He thought about what kind of person would indulge in such sloppiness. Cleaning up after yourself, especially in public, is one of the simplest ways to maintain the social contract. Amongst the multitude of moral quandaries one could be excused for misinterpreting or misremembering, the simple act of tidiness needed no more explanation or thoughtful endeavor than to simply oblige in the task itself. Common decency is common sense.

Lost in his misgivings about human nature, Charlie was startled by the sound of someone clearing their throat. It was Casey, trying to get his attention, one of her boots tapping impatiently on the worn-out linoleum floor.

"I see you've got a new tattoo," he said when he saw the freshly inked words "Keep Flying" on her thigh above an image of a derelict spaceship, a tattoo he knew well from their nights of binge-watching shows together. Those were good times, mostly, while they lasted.

"I see your eyes looking somewhere they shouldn't be," she said.

"Fair point," he acknowledged and raised his head, avoiding the cadre of tattoos covering so much of her bare skin.

She glared at him, his coffee and bagel in her hands.

"The line work is excellent, though," he said. "You have an impeccable taste for tattoo artists."

"Coffee, black and boring, with a plain and nearly tasteless bagel," she shouted for all to hear, shoving the mug in front of him, the coffee spilling onto Charlie's freshly cleaned counter space.

There were only four people in the café, and they were snickering. Charlie didn't care. He smiled as he looked into her eyes, the sky-blue irises a beautiful complement to her pale skin.

"You have a knack for the mundane," Casey offered, resting one elbow on the counter as she continued to stare disapprovingly at him.

Raising his hand like a student in a classroom, Charlie waited patiently for her to allow him to speak.

"I'm right beside you and staring directly at you," Casey said. "You can speak without being called on. I'm not your teacher."

"Yes, but your tone of voice and the glare in your eyes make you seem like an authority figure, so I thought I'd be respectful," he said.

This was his best attempt at flirting with her. He'd

never been good at it.

"Do not try to clean up that coffee until you're finished," she said as she leaned close, staring into his eyes. "Understand?"

"Yes, but—,"

"No buts. And leave a good tip!"

"I already tipped when I paid," he protested, trying to stay focused on the conversation as she walked away and his eyes were drawn to her posterior.

"You heard what I said, Charlie. And stop staring at my ass. It's not on the menu," she called out as she made her way into the kitchen.

"I was so close to not having to deal with any of this ever again," he murmured.

He made quick work of his breakfast, his worries momentarily fading while he enjoyed the quiet simplicity that followed the early-morning office-worker rush. Though a few stragglers had come in, the late-morning crowd of writers and cautiously optimistic job-seekers had yet to arrive.

Charlie had always loathed the thought of any unanticipated social contact, especially in the morning. He embraced his relative solitude while it lasted. He savored the last few bites of his bagel and his last swig of coffee. He didn't want to be alive, but for the time being, he wouldn't waste a good moment.

Before he put his empty cup on the counter, Casey stood at his side, a to-go cup in her hand.

"I was actually thinking about having a second cup

here," Charlie said, trying to smile with a debonair flair, though he knew it probably just looked like he had a facial tic from too much caffeine.

"I didn't give you shit for coming in here and having breakfast," Casey said, "but you're not getting out of your shift by hanging around and having a second cup of coffee. You need to work more because I've been to that disheveled apartment you call home and it's depressing. I wanted to jump off the balcony the last time I was there just to escape it. Plus, if you're lazy ass is late then I'll have to work longer and I'm not inclined to cover for you anymore."

"That's harsh," Charlie said. "Not entirely inaccurate, but definitely harsh. Though I would have happily joined you on the balcony had you mentioned it at the time." The thought of coming in for a shift was disheartening and unacceptable. He thought of telling her he would no longer be working there, or anywhere, but that would cause a catastrophic confrontation. Leaving in peace and never returning was his best option. Since their breakup, it's not like they talked outside of work anyway.

Casey's eyes stayed on his as he stood up and began to walk away. She cleared her throat angrily. It took him a moment to realize she had not been joking about the extra tip.

"My apologies," he stuttered, pulling his backpack around so he could get out some money for her. He was distracted and accidentally unzipped the pocket containing his unwelcome companion.

"Oh shit!" he yelled.

Luminescent water surged out of the backpack, spilling onto the floor and splashing all over him and Casey. She leaped onto the countertop, her high-top combat boots dripping wet.

"What the hell?" she shouted while Charlie fought with his backpack, trying to zip it closed.

Everyone in the coffee shop screamed as the water continued to pour out of his backpack, rushing across the floor and sweeping tables and chairs aside. Charlie finally zipped up the backpack and cut off the flow of water. He took a breath and could feel his heart racing and pounding in his chest. He looked up at Casey, her tattooed legs soaring above his empty plate and cup.

"Forgot I put that in there," he muttered.

Casey's fists were balled up and her knuckles were turning white. The rest of the wait staff burst out from the kitchen, the first two slipping in vaudevillian fashion to the floor. Charlie cringed at the sound of their bodies hitting the linoleum.

"You need to leave," Casey hissed between clenched teeth. "Now!"

Charlie slung the wet backpack around his shoulders again, feeling the water soaking into his clothes. Making gestures of apology to the customers standing on their chairs or drenched to their knees, he said, "Sorry, forgot to air it out after I washed it yesterday. You know, normal stuff." He paused at the door for one last glimpse of everyone, Casey included.

With a smile and a wave, he bolted from the café, certain he would never be allowed in again. A pleasing notion, given his desire to never work another shift. Charlie proceeded to walk homeward, avoiding the puzzled glances of pedestrians as they passed the man who was sopping wet from the knees down.

"Bullshit day. Wasn't even supposed to be alive anymore," he mumbled as he tried to retrieve his vape from his pocket.

Four

Trudging up the stairs to his apartment, his wet feet leaving soggy prints behind, Charlie muttered incessantly. His mind was racing, trying to convince him that everything he'd experienced was a fever dream. In desperate scenarios the brain releases chemicals to create a sense of calm, though his mind was choosing to take the opposite approach.

By the time he reached the eighth floor, the weight of his legs was painful. It was a steep hike to his place, and the stairwell's drab and colorless concrete walls offered little comfort. Charlie knew the elevator would've been much easier on his body, but the thought of having to see another human being within its tight confines had deterred him. No one ever took the stairs in this building.

The door to his floor was heavy as he pushed it open. In the event of fire, would a one hundred pound door made of steel be something that terrified people could pry open in time to escape a deluge of flames and smoke? Maybe, maybe not. Or maybe he needed to stop thinking so much about death.

As Charlie proceeded down the hallway to his door, he tried to ignore the stains on the dingy institutional carpet—most of them made by vomit from his neighbors' drunken escapades. The superintendent never bothered to have someone come and clean it. Since he also never replaced any of the bulbs in the hall light fixtures, Charlie didn't have to worry about seeing the floor much longer anyway.

"Back again," he whispered as his key slipped into the deadbolt. The clicks and turns of its pins offered him welcome access to the only place people were legally bound to leave him alone. "I guess I'll be here for a little while longer," he said, taking a deep drag from his vape and closing his eyes. The smell of his own home embraced him as he closed the door to the world behind him.

A change of clothes and a few hours of sleep were desperately needed, but a cleansing was required first.

He made his way to the bathroom with his backpack, dropped it in the tub to dry off, and began to pry off his jeans. They were stuck to his legs and he struggled to pull them past his ankles. Water dripped to the floor when he balled them up and squeezed them. He felt a small sense of accomplishment until he heard someone pounding on his front door. As he turned to leave the bathroom, he slipped on a wet spot and hit the floor. Frustrated, he took a swing at his backpack and nearly connected with the unicorn's horn as its head popped out of the bag.

"Unnecessary and rude," the unicorn snapped as the gushing water quickly filled the tub and spilled over the side. "We don't have time to play around. I've got a nasty situation on my hands and I need to start resolving it before the waves get out of control and form a vortex of disastrous proportion."

"What?" Charlie stumbled over Frids's words as the pounding on his door grew louder. He could hear Casey's muffled shouts.

"The multiverse, Charlie. I just had to watch a universe descend into the gravitational waves, and the flow of time and space in my dimension is getting even worse."

Before he could muster a response, Charlie heard his front door swing open and Casey's voice got even louder and more impatient.

"You've got a shitload of explaining to do!" she shouted, making her way to the bathroom. "And put your clothes on if you're naked. I'm not obligated to see that side of you anymore."

Charlie reached for his pants but only found the extended hoof of Frids.

"What the hell is this?" Casey said as she stepped into the bathroom and saw Charlie being pulled into the backpack.

He had tried to pull away from Frids, but the unicorn's surprising strength overwhelmed him. He caught a glimpse of Casey's befuddled face just as the zipper closed behind him.

Five

DEATH—IF THAT'S WHAT THIS was—felt weird.

A massive weight descended on Charlie's back as darkness surrounded him. He wasn't sure if he should or even could move. His thoughts began to drift. Had he been buried alive? There could be worse outcomes, but he wondered why he had to be awake for it. And why was he bobbing up and down?

Life had been torturous enough. Was death going to be more of the same?

"Charlie!" Frids shouted in his ear. "We don't have time to waste with you just lying there limp."

Death started to seem more appealing when Frids's hoof began pounding on his head.

Charlie felt himself being rolled and pushed until a bright light appeared. He tried to remember everything that had led up to this point. *A frequency radiating in interdimensional space*. What the hell did that even mean?

There was no time to try and answer the question as

the light grew much stronger and blinded him.

"Turn it down A-35," Frids said, ushering the glowing entity off of Charlie's back and allowing him to move. "This one's more sensitive than the last."

As the light dimmed, Charlie's sight returned. Frids came back into view, his body just as disturbing and unexplainable as he had always been. Charlie didn't understand why Frids had no tail. The unicorn had a horn—crooked and mishappen, yes, but at least it was there, resting above a feathery pink mane. Eyes, ears, and mouth— horribly scribbled on as if a child had been in charge, but at least they were present and accounted for. So why no tail?

That question went unanswered too as Charlie realized he was looking into the eyes of a sentient teddy graham, a snack he had eaten when he was young . Although this one was radiating an immense light from its sugary, bearlike body. Unlike the snack he'd devoured, this teddy graham had wildly swinging arms and legs.

"Why is there a teddy graham staring at me? Also, second thought, but equally as relevant as the first, how is there a teddy graham staring at me?"

"Charlie, meet A-35. A-35, meet Charlie. A-35 will be devouring us shortly so I can show you firsthand the issue I've been trying to resolve."

Before Charlie could put his confusion into words, he saw the bear's jaw drop open. Charlie tried to roll away. He was lying on the wooden deck of a ship in his boxers. He experienced a sense of fear and vulnerability he hadn't felt since gym class in grade school.

"Close your mouth," Frids shouted at the bear. "We're not going just yet."

The creature was just as frightening with its mouth closed. Charlie tried to avoid the outstretched arms of the walking snack as it began to chase him around the deck. Its brimming smile and welcoming eyes were terrifying. He had once seen such a look on a street corner preacher of an apocalyptic cult. Maybe that guy was right, Charlie thought to himself.

"He likes you."

Frids's opinion of the situation did not help matters. Charlie danced around the mast, looking over the side of the boat for any means of escape, but he saw nothing except black waves with sparkling crests.

"Is this hell?"

"What's hell?"

"The place I can only imagine this nightmare was formed in."

Charlie turned to see the creepy bear skipping toward him, its arms open wide. Trusting his fear more than Frids, Charlie swung his leg and kicked the bear in its stomach. It bent over and vomited a gaseous nebula that swirled around its head. Charlie grabbed it by its arms and flung it over the railing. It appeared to giggle in delight as it took flight, only to disappear in a mini-explosion as it came into contact with the water below.

His breath was hard to control. Nothing made sense. He leaned against the railing, trying to ease the sensation of wanting to vomit and pass out, hoping he wasn't going to excrete a nebula as well.

"I understand you may have been scared, but destroying an entire universe was just a massive overreaction. Can you even conceive of the trillions of lifeforms you just extinguished?" Frids said, lifting two hooves and setting them on top of the railing, standing on two tiny hindlegs.

Charlie just stared at him.

"These bears are the representation of individual universes connected by this interdimensional plane. Welcome to the multiverse, Charlie."

Pointing over the railing, Charlie tried to form a coherent question, but he could only utter a single word: "Dead?"

"No, I'm just messing with you," Frids said, chuckling. The unicorn watched the ongoing explosion of lights underneath the murky water. "Oh...actually." As the light dissipated, the unicorn got back down on four hooves, his cardboard head turning to look at the vast expanse above them, searching for something. The unicorn's head went back and forth until a glowing light appeared. "I was worried, but there it is." Frids patted Charlie on the leg then bit down on the hem of his boxers, pulling him away from the railing.

"What the fuck is happening?" Charlie shouted.

Frids sat Charlie down then trotted over to the door leading below deck and barked out an order for everyone to come up.

"Here, this should help."

Unable to imagine anything that could help, Charlie simply stared as a line of glowing bears filled the deck. They were giggling and elbowing one another as they maneuvered for space. Their glow stretched far beyond the boat.

"Are you God?" Charlie said to Frids.

"What?"

"God. Creator thing. Life force giver of stuff."

"No. That's... That's just weird. What is it that makes your species want a deity figure?"

Charlie shrugged as Frids returned his attention to the glowing and childlike bears.

"Each one of these bears represents a universe in which I've already attempted to save you from committing suicide. Each one was a failure. I've tried to reach out to you in numerous stages of your life, from your teenage years to those mere minutes before you turned thirty, the final point at which you seem to be able to exist. The multiverse allows me the opportunity to see you at every age and in every conceivable existence, but none of my attempts have worked so far."

"How have you been able to reach me at different ages? Shouldn't I be this age in all of time and space?"

Frids tapped its head with a hoof before releasing a sigh. "Don't be naïve, Charlie. Your universe operates in time and space in accordance with the physical structure it took during its creation. Other universes don't have to operate just like yours, and time can flow differently.

It's selfish to think every one of you should operate on the same timeframe. Don't be selfish, Charlie."

For a moment, Charlie was filled with a mixture of frustration and envy. All these versions of himself were able to do what he had failed at and was now being punished for. And for his failure, he was granted the gift of being talked down to by an arrogant piece of discarded cardboard.

"With each failure, the waves get worse and my ship gets harder to maintain. The different universes are somehow pulling toward one another at an exponential rate, all heading toward a single point in this plane. If we can't stop this, Charlie, they'll breach their dimensional plane in space and time and will flow into this dimension. The force of gravity they'll bring with them will tear a hole in the multiverse and create a singularity so powerful no universe will be able to resist its pull."

"So you're saying I can die and not even have to worry about this anymore."

"Not the point, Charlie. It won't just be you who dies. It will be everyone and everything. All matter will be ripped apart and destroyed, exterminating all of existence."

"And what am I supposed to do about it?"

"Help me stop it."

"How?" Charlie wasn't keen on the prospect of making any effort, but his growing fascination with the restless bears, which kept slapping and poking one another until an actual brawl broke out, was enough for him to keep the conversation going so he could watch. That is, until he glanced down and realized his scrawny legs were still bare and exposed and his boxers were dirty. "Pants!"

"Use your full vocabulary, Charlie. I stopped trying to talk to the versions of you who weren't able to at least maintain their part in a coherent conversation."

"I want pants. I have no pants. Can I please, somehow, in this horrid place of implausibility, be given a pair of pants to wear?"

"Fine." Frids stepped over to Charlie and snatched at his boxers, gripping them with its cardboard teeth.

"No, no, no!" Charlie struggled to resist the removal of his boxers until he saw the fabric was stretching and reaching all the way down to his ankles—covering his exposed skin.

"Now that your shame has been quelled, don't kill yourself?" Frids offered.

"Unlikely solution. What else you got?" He was grateful for the extension of his garments, but the situation called for no more repayment than a simple thank you. Giving in to such a high demand was not on the table.

Sitting on its hind legs, Frids tried again. "Then at least let me show you what you'll destroy along with yourself. Maybe if you see what's out in the multiverse, you'll understand that there is more to life than just you, and I will have time to salvage all of existence."

Charlie was perplexed. He had never considered

himself to be the overly selfish type and wasn't keen on the idea of exterminating all of existence, but why should he be forced to suffer? Why should he bear the weight of galaxies so others could smile and be happy while he trudged through the abyss of depression? But maybe he could see a few more sights before he found his way back to the nothingness that was calling him.

"Fuck it. Why not? I'll walk around with you for a bit. Just two questions, maybe three."

Frids bounced around in front of Charlie. "Definitely. Absolutely. This is the best I've ever done with one of you, so let's do this. Do you want to know how matter coalesced during the expansion points in the early moments of your universe? Why do the humans in your world keep saying there is a brontosaurus and then there isn't, and then there is again? Or, maybe, how you can exceed the speed of light to travel into the interdimensional plane and hang out with me when this is over?"

"Nothing so inconsequential. First, why are we on a ship that looks like it belongs in a Pirates of the Caribbean ride? Second, why in the fuck are you a cardboard unicorn with vicious teddy grahams for friends?" Charlie took a break from his line of questioning to watch one of the bears break off a piece of the railing and attempt to stab another bear with it. "And third, and maybe most importantly, why is there a massive beam of light careening toward us?"

Frids followed Charlie's eyes and looked up. "Oh,

that's A-35 coming back down. It's our first universe to go play around in."

Before Charlie could ask another question, the beam of light slammed into the ship, and just before everything went dark, he saw the creepy grin of the bear he had tossed overboard.

"Time to go!" Frids shouted, poking the bear on its forehead, releasing its jaw, and pulling Charlie into its gaping mouth.

Six

Many of Charlie's worst experiences had taken place in darkness. In the light of day, his family sometimes smiled at him. But at night their attitudes shifted, and he became the target for their release of pent-up aggression, especially his father's.

His brothers and sister, on occasion, would target him, too. Sometimes they would lock him in the windowless basement, where he struggled to find a light switch. He could hear their laughter as his fingers searched the walls. Then their laughter faded, and he tried not to cry by telling himself over and over that he would be ok. The sound of his own voice calmed him until he heard another voice shout, *No, you won't!* He thought it must be one of his brothers who had snuck back in, but he was still alone, listening to the demons inside his own mind.

Charlie remembered screaming. It was the first time he just gave up and welcomed death. He wanted to be free from life's tortures. But then a light filled the room, and he heard his father, who was angry that Charlie had ruined his quiet evening—a rare date night—with Charlie's mom.

As Charlie tried to remember his father's expression, Frids's misshapen face popped into view.

"What the hell just happened?" Charlie asked.

"That was transuniversal travel," Frids said. "Welcome to your other home in A-35. It's pretty similar to what you knew back in your personal spot in the multiverse. Thought this might be an easy beginner trip to get you used to travel before we set off and begin our search for a reason to live."

Glancing around, Charlie recognized his own apartment—the same furniture, the same walls and windows, the same knick-knacks – collectible action figures, the occasional photo, gaming systems, and a DVD collection that time had made nearly obsolete. Various Lego sets he had meticulously built sat on bookcases along the walls. He smiled, remembering the joy each construction had given him. Everything appeared to be exactly the same as his home. Were he not staring at a Frids, he would have thought he had just woken up from a dream.

"I figured the other versions of me would have different stuff," he mused as he gently touched a reconstruction of the Tokyo Tower made of Lego bricks. He had hopes of seeing it in person with Casey at his side, but this was the closest he had ever gotten.

"Some do, but not many. Unlike other people,

you—and all the versions of you in the multi-verse—nearly always make the same decisions leading to the same unfortunate outcome."

"Then what makes you think you'd be able to change any one of our minds if you haven't already?"

"Nothing ever comes from not trying."

Charlie opened the blinds, expecting to see the calm and sunny street outside his apartment complex. Instead, he saw a scene of utter destruction. Buildings were exploding or on fire, debris was flying, pedestrians were running for their lives. Small black drones flew in unison above them, releasing bombs one after the other.

"Well, this looks like a fun place to convince someone not to kill themself," Charlie said.

"Just hold on for a second," Frids answered, waving his hoof. "Let's just see if anything is going on to explain this rationally." Trotting over to the TV, Frids tapped his horn on the screen and a flood of gory images appeared above a news anchor, who was crying in horror.

"*The Cephalopod invasion is upon us! Arm yourselves with whatever weapons you have and pray to your gods that we can stop them. The president is dead and her cabinet is scattered. The armed forces are in disarray an—.*"

As the man squealed, a giant squid rushed to his desk and peeled him apart with its tentacles until there was only a puppet left to finish the broadcast.

"*To our new human pests, please know that we are*

here to only harm the majority of you. Some will live through the proceeding and unavoidable invasion. Do not be alarmed. Death is not implied with each interaction, but it will come quickly if you do not meet our specifications and standards. Thank you for your cooperation with our expanding control of the galaxy."

The squid slithered offscreen, leaving the remains of the anchor draped over the news desk, a black ooze mixing with his bones and blood. Charlie tried to process the sight as his emotions leapt from fear to bewilderment, and then back again.

"I don't want to be a Debbie Downer here, but I think if this Charlie is still alive, he should be left to make his own decisions."

"Hmm."

"What?"

"I think I know that squid?"

"Again, what?"

"You know what? I do know him. His name is Glibon. In another universe I traveled to he was actually your therapist."

"Is this a joke? Is this a bad, unnecessary joke? Feels like you're trying to be cute and say something to save your ass from dragging me into a literal hell."

"No joke. It was the first universe I went to thinking you'd have the better chance now that healthcare and all essential needs were covered by the New Cephalopod Order. Thought I would have nailed it on the first try, but you were a slippery one."

"So I was able to run away and keep you from finding me?"

"No. You were literally slippery. You jumped into a riptide and floated out to sea to drown. I tried to grab you but this cardboard doesn't offer much in terms of strength when that amount of salt water is involved."

"Now, hang on a—."

Charlie was cut off by an explosive force bursting open the door to the apartment as a screeching six-foot squid began to swarm them.

"Uh-uh. This is not how I go out!" Charlie shouted as pieces of his Lego tower sailed past his head.

"Grab my horn," Frids shouted as he opened a flap on his chest, revealing a flimsy red button atop a small cardboard box. "Re-entry into my dimension is going to be a little dicey!"

Charlie gripped Frids's horn, feeling it bend beneath his weight as a tentacle wrapped around his neck, pulling him down. He lost touch with gravity as the light faded and darkness resumed.

There was no time to think. The darkness faded quickly and his body landed on the deck of the ship amongst a smattering of glowing teddy grahams. The air was knocked out of him, and he writhed for a moment, rolling back and forth.

"Better than I expected," the unicorn said from somewhere behind him. Charlie remained splayed on the deck as Frids appeared above his face. "Thought you might have splattered on impact at the rate we came flying back in," Frids said. "Good job on not dying, Charlie."

"I want to kill you," Charlie said, his voice barely audible as his lungs fought for a breath of air. He braced his palms on the deck and tried to lift himself up. There was a severed tentacle beside him. The giant squid had tried to latch onto him, but Charlie somehow managed to hurl it overboard.

"That's unnecessary," Frids said, "but I'll consider your complaint when I plan our next journey into another universe. I was already thinking of a few others we could try and asked B-15 and Q-11 to prep themselves for entry. I even double-checked to make sure that there was no chance of a cephalopod invasion that could kill you."

Arrogance was always an immediate turn-off for Charlie. No matter who it was—a girlfriend or a friend—the moment Charlie sensed excessive arrogance, he would walk away from the relationship. Frids's unmistakable self-importance made him want to vanish from the interdimensional being's presence.

"I want you to return me to my home and never come see me again."

Locked in a staring contest he could never win, Charlie pushed against the deck and slowly lifted himself up. He kicked away the glowing bears that swarmed his legs and strode past Frids. His mind was set. He had no desire to remain on this ship, no matter how fantastical it seemed. Everything about it seemed like figments of his childhood imagination, and he had too many scars to want to revisit that era of his life.

"Charlie, I didn't come to torture or endanger you. I'm not being facetious or coy when I say your life is a linchpin in the continued existence of the multiverse. It's a fact I've worked out, and I can show you empirical data to prove it."

"I don't care! I don't care about my universe. I don't care about any other universe. I don't care what your expectations of me are in your little plan. I listened to you. I joined you on an adventure, and now I'm ready to go home and get back to the business that you ripped me away from."

Frids's demeanor changed. The unicorn's head hung low as he said, "Follow me," and led Charlie up some stairs toward the helm of the ship.

Charlie could feel a sliver of regret pushing its way through his anger. A part of him wanted to stay—but he refused to give in to it. The sense of adventure he had longed for was within his grasp but his fear dominated his intrigue.

He bounded up the stairs behind Frids, taking them two at a time. When he reached the upper deck, he found Frids standing above a small hatchway, a forlorn look on its assembled face.

"You can use this hatch to return home," Frids said. "But I can't do this without you, Charlie."

Charlie's pang of regret came back but he didn't dare express it. "Find another me."

Frids opened the hatch, stepping to the side to allow Charlie access. For a brief moment Charlie wanted the unexplainable to continue. His youthful desires for fantastic experiences pushed through the recesses of his mind. Would he really throw away all that he had always longed for and give in to melancholy?

But he had not anticipated the inescapable draw of the open hatch. Charlie's legs were pulled toward the opening, and before he could take another breath, he was sucked into the dark.

Seven

THE TUB WAS COLD. Charlie could feel the inch or so of water in it soaking through the jeans he was now wearing. He got out of the tub and looked around the bathroom. He felt safe. He was home. The visions of unknown worlds were quickly dissipating as he began to settle into the familiar reality he had been born into.

His backpack was propped up inside the tub, fully zipped and motionless. He suppressed the urge to open it and see if Frids was inside. Solitude was becoming more appealing as adventure crept further and further away. Why ruin it with curiosity?

For the second time today, he disrobed. This time, he wasn't interrupted. He was free to do as he pleased. He removed the backpack from the tub and turned on the shower, letting the water slowly heat up. He stared at himself in the mirror and saw his tired eyes and face. He couldn't really blame his haggard appearance on the events of the last few hours, because this image was too familiar.

His hair was shaggy and needed a trim. His apathy had kept him from completing even the simple task of walking into a barber shop for a haircut. The bulge in his stomach was a reminder of his recent lack of exercise. He had once trained himself to run on a constant basis, trimming the fat from his body and experiencing moments of elation as he raced across finish lines. He couldn't remember why he had stopped running as he poked at his fleshy gut.

"Hello old friend," he whispered to himself. A twinge of depression turned into a powerful wave.

Tears dripped down his cheeks. He wasn't supposed to be alive right now. It had taken so much strength and determination to stick to his plan before, and now he had to start all over again. Now he would be stuck with the task of purging the nonsense his brain had been filled with of the multiverse.

But why? Charlie argued with himself. Why not try to experience all that the multiverse has to offer? Why not stay around long enough to find a place in this universe that might bring peace and happiness?

Charlie reminded himself of the struggles he'd had as a child. His teenage years were wrought with failures. He had tried to assimilate with other kids but always managed to find himself on the outskirts of acceptability. He wasn't sure what he had done wrong.

In high school, he convinced himself that college would bring him a renewed passion for life. But once he got there, he was overcome with crippling anxiety.

There were too many people and too many responsibilities. He forced himself to socialize, and even built a few friendships. But the pressure kept building until he made his first attempt to end his life.

He could still see the empty bottle of pills in his hand. He could still hear the faint sound of sirens. He could still feel the shame of not being able to stand up to his fears.

Charlie stepped into the shower and the warm water rushed all over him. He remembered how hard it was to return to his classes after he left the hospital. He'd pushed everyone away. His anxiety grew worse, and he dropped out of college and moved back in with his parents.

His parents had doted on him in the hospital, but that soon changed. Suicide wasn't something the good people of their community did, and they started to feel a creeping sense of shame about him. And then they started to resent him.

They thought he had taken the coward's way out.

He pressed his head against the shower tiles as his spirit sank deeper. He had not been a coward. He wanted to resolve the matter on his own terms. He had taken initiative and planned his exit with precision. No one seemed to understand why he couldn't just pretend that the world is normal and life is easy. Soon after, left his parent's house to live on his own- they were too eager to remind him of the shame they felt.

His brothers and sister had cared about him. They

had visited him in the hospital to joke and lift his spirits. But their lives had expanded – marriage and kids became their priorities.

Charlie yearned to let his body disappear with the water down the drain, but he needed sleep. He needed to rest his brain and figure out what to do.

Turning off the shower, he opened the curtain and stepped onto the floor mat, grabbing a towel from beneath the sink. The mirror was shrouded in steam so he couldn't see himself, which was fine with him.

He opened the bathroom door and felt the touch of cool air. It was unpleasant but unavoidable.

Charlie took a couple of steps and stopped. Something was different, and his mind was trying to figure out what.

"Get some sleep," Casey called from the kitchen. "We can talk when you're ready." She was reading a book, a cup of tea on the table in front of her.

He was overtaken by emotion—anger, joy, fear, and embarrassment—and he could only nod at her as he slipped into his bedroom. He closed the door and made his way to bed, sinking under the blankets and letting his body and mind dissolve into the nothingness they so desired.

Eight

It was beautiful. He was adrift in a luminous dream. Bright nebulas circled his hands, newborn stars swirling around his fingers and nipping at his skin. The larger stars became unstable and exploded into supernovas.

Star dust swirled around his body, drifting into the shimmering nebula that was expanding around and inside him. A gaseous state replaced his heart and lungs, fueling him with a power far greater than his own.

He felt reborn, unbounded by the physical limitations he had become accustomed to. His existence was buoyed by the pure essence of life untainted by material desires. It was extraordinary even though he knew it was just a dream.

Then the nebula began to drift away from him, pulled into the expanse beyond his reach by a mysterious gravitational force. He was being tugged in the opposite direction. He tried to scream, to protest and prevent this unwanted departure. But nothing could be done. The nebulous state was gone.

Now before him was a vision of himself. A sullen look on his face as he idly thumbed through Lego pieces for the Millennium Falcon while sitting on his bed. Casey had picked it out, and they had spent many nights building it, hoping the finished product would become their masterpiece.

He watched as the vision of his past self slowly dug through a small bag, looking through a few thousand pieces to find the right one. It was a difficult process and required a level of patience he had struggled to acquire.

Suddenly, the bag flew across the room and slammed into the wall. Pieces scattered everywhere, littering the room with a broken sense of completion. He heard the distant voices of shouting. It was his own voice. The words were echoing around the room, remnants of the argument left behind from the moments that transpired before the vision of himself had wandered into its current state. He had been shouting at Casey - her voice responding with the same frustration and anger before the echo of a door slammed shut. She had left him.

Charlie watched as the vision of himself on the bed gripped the bag angrily before sending it flying across the room. It smashed into the wall, breaking open and scattering the pieces across the carpet. He had tried to forget this moment. He stared helplessly as the vision of himself stomped around the room. All was silent, but he didn't need to hear the shouting – he remembered the anger that convinced him to give up that night.

He closed his eyes on the vision to block out the pain. He didn't want to relive any more mistakes. But no matter how tightly he squeezed his eyelids shut, light seemed to find a way to pass through.

Opening his eyes again, Charlie found himself lying in his bed, light beaming through the windows. He crawled out from under the sheets and stared at the box beneath his bed – the Millennium Falcon secure in the spot he left it in after she left. A brief notion to pull it out to begin assembling passed through his thoughts before he let it slip away.

Nine

"So where do we begin?" Casey asked. She was being patient. It was one of the qualities Charlie found most attractive about her. She knew how hard it was for him to express himself.

His eyes focused on the mug of coffee on the table in front of him so he could avoid Casey's gaze. It had taken him a few moments to remember she was there when he first woke up; fortunately, he hadn't walked out of his bedroom naked. Now he was dressed in a pair of sweatpants and a sweatshirt, the hood pulled up over his head.

"How long was I asleep?" he asked.

The sun was shining brightly through his windows, but all the clocks were unplugged. Casey had made a habit of unplugging them when they were dating. She didn't want him worrying about the time he was wasting by not being able to be normal and function properly. He had reached that low point again, and she was trying to keep him from focusing on anything other than himself.

"Long enough for me to watch every episode of *Fire-fly*," she said. "Didn't get to watch *Serenity*, though. I'm going to have to complete the binge later at home."

"What?" Charlie looked up from his coffee to see her snickering.

"What yourself. I have no regrets from binging on a great show while you lay passed out." She took a sip of coffee. "Maybe I regret not sleeping through the night, but I have plenty of time to catch up on sleep now."

The thought of her watching over him while he slept was appealing, although the thought of her not waking him up to indulge in their favorite pastime as a couple was frustrating. "Do you not have to work today?"

"Funny thing about that," she said. "When someone you were involved with comes into work and floods it, causing the store to be shut down while a water and sewage remediation company comes in to fix the damage, you tend to get fired, too."

Charlie couldn't talk. He was remembering the world Frids had whisked him away to. He could still feel the sensation of the giant squid's tentacles grasping his body.

"Oh no, Casey. I'm *so sorry* I ruined your job," she said sarcastically as he struggled for words. "No, no. It's fine, Charlie. I'm not so keen on paying my rent, and I'm sure the landlord will be more than happy to let me stay for a month or two while I try to find a new job and build a stable life again."

"I am sorry," he said.

"I wouldn't be here if I didn't think you were. Now please tell me what the fuck is going on? They think you may have busted the main line somehow, but we both know that's not true. I watched you open that backpack."

He had no desire to reveal the insanity he had been thrust into, but she gave no quarter for an appeal to change the subject. He took a long sip from his mug and let the hot liquid fill his mouth before he swallowed. He pulled the hoodie off his head and ran his fingers through his messy hair. He could tell it was sticking out in every direction.

"I went up to the peak at Turnbolt—."

"Goddammit, Charlie!" Casey's words came out harshly as she stood up and dragged her chair toward his, sitting down so close that her knees touched his. "I told you that you could still call me if it got that bad again."

He stared down at her legs, his eyes tracing the outlines of her tattoos, aching to caress her thigh and pull her into his arms. But the time in which he could do that was gone.

"I'm not your problem to look after," he said.

"You were never my problem to look after. Not then and not now, but that doesn't mean I don't care."

An annoying little voice interrupted them. "Is this a bad time? I feel like this is a bad time, but your species is a little weird and hard to read."

Casey looked around as Charlie let his head fall to the table with a thud.

"Charlie. What the hell is that?"

Without lifting his head, Charlie lifted his arm and pointed at Frids. "Casey, this is Frids. Frids, this is Casey."

Frids's scribbled eyes locked onto Casey. "Oh, I didn't recognize this version of you."

"There's a unicorn made out of cardboard talking to me, Charlie. What the fuck did you put in your coffee, Charlie? You know I don't like to be high, Charlie!"

Casey's words got louder as she grabbed his sweatshirt and lifted his head off the table.

"You're not high, and the unicorn is real," he said. "Apparently, the multiverse is a thing, and this," Charlie waved his hand at Frids, "this is the thing that exists in the interdimensional plane that connects each universe and it's here to torment me."

"Well, that is just a fantastic explanation as to why I'm seeing a goddamn walking, talking, cardboard unicorn, Charlie!"

"It's more like a frequency radiating in interdimensional space," the unicorn interjected, "but you can call me Frids if you'd like."

"No, I do not like. I do not like at all. I'm not crazy. Talking to things like you is what crazy people do, and I've been taking meds for years to not be crazy."

"Not to say that you are crazy, but your tone certainly isn't—."

"Shut up, Frids!" Charlie shouted, trying to stop the unicorn before he could spark any more fear and anger in Casey. "You're not helping the situation." Standing up, he placed his hands on Casey's shoulders and gently pushed her back into her seat as she stared at the unicorn. "This thing appeared to me on top of the mountain the other night and stopped me, regrettably." Charlie let the last word linger as he glared at Frids, who calmy sat down beside them with a smile.

"We're best friends now," Frids added, his comment met with indifference as Charlie focused on Casey.

"I honestly have no idea how to explain it any more than that," Charlie said.

"Not a problem, Charlie." Frids leapt onto the table and knocked both of their mugs over, the coffee spilling onto the floor. "I can take it from here."

"What the hell did you do, Charlie?" Casey asked.

"He was being a little extra self-murdery throughout the multiverse, so I decided to step in and do something about it to save all of existence. According to the literature of this world I'd be classified as a hero. It's an odd terminology your people tend to throw around freely, but I think it accurately describes me."

Casey looked back and forth from Frids to Charlie, impatiently waiting for him to speak. "Charlie, explain."

Charlie reached into his pockets for his vape, pulling it out to take a long drag. Casey grabbed it from his hands before he could even finish exhaling and began taking quick drags. Charlie saw her hand trembling.

"I honestly don't know how to."

"Oh!" Frids shouted before hopping off the table, his hooves splashing into a puddle of coffee. "I can make a diagram. One of the other versions of Charlie loved diagrams so I got pretty good at them before he killed himself. Where's your arts and crafts room?"

Charlie couldn't speak. The question was too absurd. His apartment contained a bedroom and a bathroom with a small living and dining space between them. It didn't take more than a cursory glance to see the extent of it.

"Don't worry. I'll find it on my own. You two talk amongst yourselves while I prepare the presentation."

Frids darted off into Charlie's bedroom, where they could hear him tearing it apart.

"I don't think I want to be here anymore," she said.

"Replaying an old hit, I see." Charlie couldn't stop the words before they spilled out of his mouth. He saw the anger in her eyes just before he felt her hand slap his cheek.

"I'm not here to be derided for making the decision to keep myself protected."

"You were never in danger," Charlie couldn't help but say. He didn't want to fight, but his rational brain was clouded with embarrassment.

"You still have no idea what you were doing to me!" she shouted.

"It wasn't about you. I never pushed it on to you."

"No, you just pushed me away but wanted me to stay and watch you slowly dissolve until one day I would come over from work to find you dead in the bathtub."

Charlie couldn't argue with her. He had thought their relationship would push away his pain, and it did, but just for a short time. His inability to function began to weigh them down, forcing her into the role of therapist. He knew it was wrong. He knew she needed help, too. Her own struggles with depression and anxiety had been hard enough for her to deal with.

"I'm sorry," he said sincerely.

"I'm not here to rehash—."

"Diagram time!" Frids bounded back toward the table, a piece of paper clutched between his cardboard teeth.

Frids dropped the paper in front of Casey. On it was a crude drawing of Charlie with a gun to his head, a teddy graham trying to devour him, and Frids wearing a pirate hat and eye patch. All three were perched precariously on a rickety ship.

"Make sense now?" the unicorn asked, climbing into her lap and putting his face up to hers as he waited patiently for a response.

"Perfect sense." Her sarcasm fell flat on Frids.

"Great! Now, if you'll be on your way. I need Charlie's eyes on our goal and not your body."

"Fuck it. I'm out." Casey walked past Frids and tossed Charlie's vape into his lap without another glance. "I don't know what the hell this is, but I'm not diving in any deeper."

"You don't have to—," Charlie said, the slamming door catching him off guard, "go."

Seeing her walk out brought back his pain. He loved her. She was weird and beautiful. She had accepted him—all of him—and even tried to listen and understand as he explained the terror that was in his mind. And she was gone, again.

Charlie sat in silence. Frids's crude drawing rested on the table, slowly discoloring from the remnants of spilled coffee. He chuckled as the stain on the paper came near the rickety ship. Then he began to laugh, tears swelling in his eyes and slowly forcing their way out. He couldn't stop the surge of anger and sadness.

"What's wrong with me?" he asked.

"I don't know," Frids replied.

Frids sat at his side. The unicorn's natural exuberance had dissipated after Casey left. Despite the permanent expression of joy on Frids's face, his voice now held disappointment.

Wiping his eyes, Charlie tried to regain his composure, but it was futile.

"When I first met her," he said, "I thought I could make it past all of this. I thought that things would get better once I felt what it was like to be happy and comforted by someone who cared about me. But it didn't last. No matter what I did, no matter what she said, the pain always came creeping back. It never let me be content. Not once."

Charlie stood up and grabbed the back of his chair, throwing it at the wall. The sheetrock cracked from the impact. He stared at the broken chair on the floor. Maybe it could be fixed. More likely it was just trash to be thrown out.

He heard a scuffling sound and turned to see Frids dragging his backpack across the living room carpet.

"I don't know what happened," Frids said, his voice muffled by the strap in his mouth, "but I do know one way that we can try to figure it out."

Ten

Luminous gravitational waves rocked the ship. Charlie stood quietly on the deck, watching the waves rise and fall. Each one climbed up as if it ached to overtake the ship, only to be pulled back down before it could reach the deck. They yearned for something greater than what was possible. Their limitations were painful to watch.

As the deck creaked and groaned with each rise and fall of the ship, Charlie stared at the miniature teddy grahams roaming around, hurling swords at one another, and giggling when they landed in their targets. The fever dream he had been dropped into was inconceivable yet somehow existed.

Lost in thought, Charlie was startled by Frids, who was mumbling to himself as he laid a makeshift map on the deck with the word "Multiverse" scribbled in large letters at the top.

"Mind sharing your insights into the scribbled mess you've made," Charlie said.

Frids looked up from the map, his goofy smile the same as it was the first time Charlie saw him. Taking a puff from his vape and letting the water vapor linger long enough in his throat to nearly choke him, Charlie slowly let it seep from his lips.

"You're a disaster, Charlie."

"Thank you." He offered a mocking bow before taking another drag from his vape.

"But you should still be able to live. Many people in all the universes are walking disasters who affect the lives of everyone around them. But they still seem to have the ability to carry on, maintaining the cosmic average of natural and self-inflicted death."

"And your insight would be?" Charlie let the question dangle, leaving ample room for Frids to give a hopefully intelligible answer.

Frids grabbed a corner of the map between his scribbled teeth, dragging it onto Charlie's lap for closer observation.

"You see the little bright universes circling the edge of the map?"

Charlie let his eyes drift from Frids to the map. The chunky marks from the crayons Frids used were still fresh on the page, their aroma flooding him with memories of the coloring books he used to spend so much time with as a child. If he ever found some semblance of normalcy after all this, he would need to reacquaint himself with a box of crayons and a coloring book.

"What about them?"

"The space above this ship is supposed to be filled with them."

It wasn't. Charlie couldn't help but remember the vast darkness with only a smattering of light that stretched above him when he was out on the deck the first time Frids thrust him into this interdimensional realm of insanity. In all manners of science fiction, those explorers traveling through unknown sectors of inter-galactic space always seemed to be surrounded by nebulas, exploding supernovas, and other vague yet verifiable oddities of the universe.

"Where are they?"

"Gone. The specks of light that should be above are universes I've lost contact with. If I can't connect with them, I have no chance of trying to reach that version of you to stop this. Those universes have now become susceptible to destruction - each one potentially adding to the disheveled nature of my interdimensional plane. Your exponentially increasing rate of suicide through-out the multiverse is closing off my ability to keep the multiverse alive. This is why I need your help. This is why I need you to understand the consequences of your actions. If I can break the cycle in one universe then it will show that this trend is reversible."

Charlie had taken part in many unnecessarily de-ranged conversations in his life. Working retail on a Black Friday had shown him the insanity that could overtake people considered to be normal when given a twenty-percent-off deal.

Frids's hope was appealing, though. Charlie loved this kind of optimism and fought for its warmth on many occasions. He had even been given glimpses of its power over despair. But he could never sustain a positive outlook for very long, and its power dwindled away from him over time, leaving him staring into an abyss.

"But isn't there an infinite number of me out there? How could infinity reach zero?"

"Zero is the gravitational center of all numbers. It's the fulcrum that binds the positive and the negative. And the further they reach out, the faster they fall back in when compromised. Infinity has its limits, Charlie."

"No. Infinity is infinity."

"No. Infinity has levels, and you're collapsing them."

"Math sucks."

"You suck, Charlie. You suck."

It was clear that he had struck a nerve. Frids poked his leg with his bent horn.

"Thanks for the kind words," Charlie said.

"You're not welcome. Look, you know how to count from zero to one, right?"

"Yes." Charlie shook his head, weary of the tone so many had taken with him throughout his life, thinking that they needed to dumb everything down to its simplest point.

"In between zero and one is a set of numbers stretching on into infinity."

"But," Charlie groaned, taking a drag on his vape and releasing a plume of vapor into the air.

"But you know both one and zero are their own separate entities. One contains a specific value, and zero contains no value. You, throughout the multiverse, equals one. You, exponentially killing yourself throughout the multiverse, is leading to zero—and the collapse of all existence."

"You've already talked about this, and I told you before, I don't care."

Putting his front hooves up on Charlie's knees, Frids forced his head into Charlie's view. "You might not care about yourself, but you do care about life, maybe not for yourself but for others around you. I watched you talking to Casey. I've watched you, dozens of times now in different universes, talking to her. I'm sure there are universes out there where you loathe her, but in the vast majority, you want her to be happy, with or without you."

"Fuck you." Charlie pushed Frids away before standing up, watching the unicorn struggle to right himself on the deck.

"They're going to die. Every incarnation, every memory, every aspect of their touch on this multiverse will blink out along with all that exists around them."

"I'm not the one who's doing this to me. I'm the one who's suffering through it. You say you've seen multiple versions of me and that they're all tortured by the same suicidal thoughts. Why don't you figure out who or what is trying to destroy me instead of blaming me for it? I've tried being positive and living life with joy. I desperately want to be happy and enjoy the things that the rest of the world gets to enjoy with apparent ease. The only thing that has kept me from trying to kill myself on a daily basis has been my fierce determination that there must be a better life than this."

Charlie wanted to storm off to the escape hatch but thought better of it when he saw two rows of glowing bears lining up, donning pirate hats and eye patches as if preparing for battle.

"This whole place," he said, "is fucking crazy."

"It's not meant to be," Frids responded. "My existence depends on stability here. I have no real corporeal form, nor was I ever meant to interact with any life. I'm just supposed to be an intermediary between the different universes so they stay connected until they end."

"Well, if they're all going to end, then why stop me? It's going to happen one day anyway, with or without me alive."

"Universes die, Charlie. Not the multiverse. All matter can be repurposed to spawn another universe so long as the whole stays stable. If the whole becomes unstable, they all begin collapsing in on one another until they coalesce in an inescapable space."

"I just want to die. I'm not asking for the whole universe to join me."

"You don't get that option, Charlie. And I think I know why."

"I don't care. I'm not an experiment for you to play

with that makes you feel better about yourself when you solve the puzzle. I have control over nothing but myself. You don't have the right to take that away."

Frids stared at Charlie quietly before trotting over and embracing Charlie's leg with two hooves.

"Ew, no. This is a no. I don't hug."

"Oh, sorry," Frids replied, backing away. "Misread the moment there."

"A little bit, yeah."

The two were quiet for a moment, embarrassed by the awkward hug. Frids finally broke the silence.

"You aren't the puzzle, Charlie. Who you are, what you do, that is all your decision. But the reason for this continuous descent into despair and suicide is linked to something greater beyond you. That's what I'm looking to solve."

"Like...like a god?"

"What? No. Again with the deity stuff. Stop it," Frids said, pounding on the deck with a hoof, though it barely made a sound. "Stop it."

Charlie threw his hands up in surrender. He had never felt concerned with the existence of some greater being, but when presented with the cosmically inconceivable, anything can seem at least fractionally plausible.

"My working theory is that every universe begins with the rapid expansion of matter and heat."

"Like the Big Bang?"

"Weird way to describe it, but sure, the big bang.

During the first fraction of a second, there exists an imbalance of matter and antimatter. In each universe, one always wins since the two can't co-exist in the same space. The destructive power that's wielded when the two collide at the atomic level is enough to destroy each other."

"Totally makes sense. I'm following every word you're saying," Charlie said, his sarcasm lost on Frids, who looked pleased with Charlie's response.

"That's good, but I see no need for your interruption then."

"Please, do carry on," Charlie insisted, "but could you lend me a pen and pad? I'd like to take notes for the test at the end."

"Don't be cynical, Charlie. You don't have enough charisma for people to like you when you're being cynical."

"Maybe you can poof some charm into my attitude then, asshole."

"I'm not magical, Charlie. I'm not a real unicorn. I'm a representation of one."

"Oh, my apologies. Wait," Charlie said, his mind shifting from derision to actual intrigue, "do you unicorns really exist?"

"Pay attention, Charlie. This is the multiverse. Of course unicorns exist. Now, as I was saying, during this rapid expansion of each universe, I think there must be subatomic remnants of anti-matter left behind that must've pulled together over billions of years until they were finally able to inhabit a life form from which they could wreak havoc."

"I feel like what you're saying is that I'm a big bomb waiting to go off, but what I care about right now is the fact that unicorns exist and I'm potentially in a position to go see them."

"You don't care about anything I'm saying right now, do you?" Frids's voice was becoming frayed as he slumped to the deck. "You just want to go see a unicorn."

"I do, yes. I'd like to go see a unicorn, please."

"If I promise to take you to see a universe in which unicorns are in abundance, will you first let me run my experiment to verify my theory that there is antimatter residue resting within your molecular structure? And also, could you promise to not kill yourself? I don't think either of these is too much to ask."

"As long as you promise to not contort and dismember my body, we can run your test. But I think we both know it's a 50/50 proposition at best that I won't commit suicide." The excitement of seeing a real life unicorn was washing over the despair. He was still a child desperate to believe in magic.

Frids perked up and began hopping around the deck. "Make it a 60/40 proposition and I'll get you to a unicorn."

How simple it was to lie. With a smile, he ignored his cynical desire to argue the statistical probability of his impending suicide. "Sure thing," Charlie said. "It's

most certainly a 60/40 one now that you've asked nice-
ly."

"Ha! I knew I was getting better at this," Frids said
excitedly. "Now let's get that brain under a microscope
and cut it open just a little bit."

"No, no, no. We agreed to no cutting or dismember-
ing. You try to come at me with any sharp objects and I
will set fire to this whole ship and every damn bear on
it."

"No need to resort to the psychotic, Charlie. I was
only kidding...mostly. Now come and follow me."

Charlie began to regret his compliance. He could still
leave, still avoid being under the microscope of an even
greater insanity than his own. But curiosity compelled
him to follow the unicorn. "Why not?"

Eleven

It was raucous below the deck. Glowing bears were running rampant, chasing each other in a bizarre frenzy. They were like children playing tag. Their innocence reminded Charlie of running around in the sun with his siblings. Despite the pain they could inflict when in the mood to torment him, they would still play with him in the afternoons before dinner. He had good and bad memories of them, and he wasn't sure which ones to keep close.

"Why do they act this way?" he asked as a bear leaped through the air to tackle another. It missed and landed with a thud. Picking itself back up, it giggled and continued its pursuit.

"Most universes are still relatively young. Their life spans can stretch for trillions of years, even after all life that can exist within them has perished. Had I not built in the hatch for you to return home, you would have seen yours just as bright and brilliant playing amongst the others. It might be hard to comprehend but they are the equivalent of cosmic children."

"It must become lonely for them after all life has died within their universe," Charlie said. He didn't understand where his empathy for them came from, but he understood the concept of loneliness far too well.

"It does. You aren't the only thing that wishes you could die when life appears to be pointless."

"How do they die? Can they even die?"

"All life dies, Charlie. The energy in each universe slowly seeps away until it can no longer hold its structure. That's when it falls into my realm and I disperse its remains back into the multiverse to begin anew."

"So you're like an interdimensional grim reaper?"

"I'm a conduit for energy disbursement. The multiverse is dependent on being restructured and revitalized with new universes that populate and support its structure."

They stopped in front of a door with a loosely hanging sign on which was scribbled, "Lab and Stuff." Its rudimentary appearance was not reassuring.

"So what happens when you die?" Charlie asked.

Frids paused, his hoof resting on the door. "I wish I knew. I know I'll die. Everything dies eventually, but I've never seen what comes after or what came before. I still wish I knew, though."

The thought that even such a being as Frids was unable to know what came after life was disconcerting. Charlie had accepted that it likely ended in nothingness but that didn't take away the sinking feeling in his stomach.

Stepping into the room, Charlie saw that the walls were lined with an array of screens covered with bouncing and beeping dots. Vials full of unknown substances were shaking crazily on the opposite side of the room. On the walls were drawings of nebulas and planets, comets and asteroids. It was a beautiful mural of matter coalescing throughout space.

"Go ahead and lie down on the table," Frids said, "while I get everything situated for the test. It should only take a couple of minutes for the instruments to be prepared."

Frids stepped past Charlie and began tapping on the nearest screen. An image of Mario appeared, the bright white words "Level 1-1" flashing on the screen as Mario began running through the 2-D world. The soundtrack of his 8-bit youth began ringing in his ears and he remembered the sweet melody of rainy days spent in front of a side-scrolling world of wonder.

"Your instruments are a video game?" Charlie asked uneasily as he lay down on the table.

"The construct of this ship is based around the thoughts and images of your conscious matter. It's used to make it appear familiar and comforting. Within the embedded images are my means of assessing your internal structure."

"You just got killed by a Goomba."

Frids looked at the screen and tapped it with his bent horn, resetting it. "Sorry. Sometimes it takes a little reset to get it working properly."

"You can always take out the cartridge and blow on it," Charlie said.

"That seems unnecessary and unproductive," Frids said, again oblivious to Charlie's sarcasm. They both watched as Mario began scrolling across the screen again. This time the figure jumped ahead and smashed his rivals. "There we go. Now go ahead and lie down on the table, Charlie, while I get the microscope loaded."

Charlie's hand was suddenly resting on a wooden board suspended in the air. The glowing bears filed in and lined up along the walls with giddy smiles. Everything was ridiculous and Charlie couldn't think properly. He climbed onto the table, resisting the urge to walk over to the game and try to find his princess. He wondered if he were able to defeat Bowser, would he find a rendition of Casey waiting for him at the end?

Frids stumbled back and forth, knocking his instruments around. Charlie grumbled in displeasure, staring at a cardboard box that seemed to be pulsing, hovering in the air high above him. A gaseous substance was seeping from its corners. Then a light started shining just above the box, beaming inside it and causing the gas to swirl into a double helix structure.

"This doesn't seem very safe," Charlie said.

"Nonsense."

Frids's words offered little comfort as Charlie heard a strange mechanical sound behind his head. Tilting his head back, he caught a glimpse of a glowing drill bit coming toward his skull. "Why is this coming toward me?" he yelled. "I don't feel like this should be coming toward me. Frids, make this thing stop coming toward me."

"It's not there to hurt you," Frids assured him. "It just needs to connect with your brain waves to monitor the gases as they make their way through your body and interact with your molecular structure."

A sudden warmth washed over Charlie, and his skin began to prickle as the gas seeped into his skin. The box was closing in on him, but he could still hear the cadence of Mario's jumps and stomps, and the triumphant tune of his 2-D icon sliding down the flagpole at the end of the first level.

The box burst with specks of light, and the gas began to swirl, forming a vortex that lifted his head off the table. The drill connected with the base of his neck, forming a comfortable support for his head.

"Well, that seems overly dramatic for a head rest!" Charlie shouted. "So is it just a head rest, or is it going to pry my head open? I'm feeling a little insecure at the moment."

There was no response. Either Frids was ignoring him, or sound couldn't pass through the box. He tried to hear the calming sound of the video game, but he heard nothing apart from the beating of his heart and his uneven breath.

He tried to contain his terror of being confined in a small space. It was a finely tuned terror he had carried with him since his youth. In one of their cruel moments, his siblings had trapped him inside a cardboard box and pretended to tape it shut. For every good memory they had made with him, there always seemed to be an agonizing one to accompany it.

Trying to slow his breath and racing heart, Charlie focused on what was in front of him instead of what was in his past. The vortex above him had a calming presence, and it seemed familiar. As his breathing eased, he remembered seeing something like it in a middle-school astronomy workbook.

"Saturn," he whispered.

The vortex turned into an exact replica of the mysterious shape that can be found on either pole of the planet with spectacular rings. It had been formed by jet streams of enormous power, and Charlie had always wondered what it would be like to fall into their grip. Would they take him to the planet's surface, or would they take him to a world unknown? He had seen reruns of the old TV show *Land of the Lost* and had dreamed that the jet streams were somehow a portal that could take him to such a place.

He was so entranced by the image above him, he couldn't look away. But when the box began to lift, he heard the raucous giggling of the glowing bears and then he saw them still standing against the wall. His eyes moved toward the screen at his side where Mario was watching Bowser cackle in despair as he fell into a pit of fire. Then he ran toward his princess. Charlie held his breath, hoping to see Casey waiting for him but Princess Peach stood where she always had, waiting for her Mario to rescue her.

"Charlie?" Frids's voice interrupted his peaceful state. "You still with me?"

"Yeah." He sat up on the table. Beautiful Saturn was gone, along with the swirling gases and the sense of peace that it had brought. "Just got lost in thought."

"That was my intention, and it paid off." Frids was peering intently at the screen in front of him.

Charlie eased himself off the table so he could see it better. "What are we looking at?" He had expected to see another video game playing out in front of the unicorn; F-Zero or Super Mario Kart, perhaps. Nothing so enjoyable appeared on the screen, though.

"This is your dysfunction."

A series of straight blue lines raced across the screen until their perfect symmetry was disrupted by a jagged ripple that forced them to crash into one another before resuming course.

"Why does it do that?" Charlie asked.

"It shouldn't do that. That is a mistake caused by a tug on the molecular structure of your brain, one that disorients the paths of your thoughts. Normal brain function doesn't bend like this."

"So I'm broken."

"Yes. But this information shows that you can be fixed. These distortions can only be caused by the antimatter residue affecting you."

"Ok. Well then, fix me. Straighten out the lines and pull that shit out of me."

Frids stepped away from the screen and headed toward the bears, ushering them out the door. "It's not that simple, Charlie. If I just pull it out, there will be nothing standing in its way, preventing it from destroying all of existence. It needs to be restrained and made dormant somehow so it doesn't spread further."

"That doesn't sound like you're going to fix me," Charlie said. "That sounds like you intend to leave it inside me. That's not what we agreed to."

"And that's not what I intend to do. I can find a way to fix this, Charlie. And now that I have more information, I can use it to find out how."

Charlie followed Frids out of the makeshift laboratory. "I don't understand."

"Neither do I, yet. But the multiverse is vast and full of answers to questions. We just need to look harder as we go through it."

"I'm not so sure I want to anymore." The disheartening resolution of Frids's experiment was crushing Charlie's hopes. The reason for his chronic bouts of pain and anguish was clear now. The culprit was inside him and he could do nothing about it.

"But you must," Frids said. "I can't go back on a promise, and I promised to take you to see the unicorns. Let's clear our heads with a little adventure and try to find something along the way that will light our path to knowledge."

"Fine," Charlie said. He knew he would regret not taking the chance to see the unicorns. "But I make no promises after that."

Twelve

Even chaos can be amusing, Charlie thought as he surveyed the commotion on deck. The glowing bears were stabbing each other with swords and laughing at the sparkling ooze that spilled out of their bodies. Maybe Frids was in control of them, but he clearly was not a hovering parent.

"C-27, leave Q-5 alone and get back into position," Frids said loudly. "F-11, take your position at the back with the anchor."

The former request was ignored, but F-11 obliged. The bear was enormous in comparison to the others, its head nearly reaching Charlie's chest while the others barely reached to his thighs. As it waddled past its brethren, Charlie thought it must be the oldest.

He fought a growing urge of hunger. He had loved teddy grahams as a child and couldn't help but want a handful right now. The bagel at the café was the last meal he had, and he had no idea how long ago that had been. Maybe time didn't matter in this dimension, but hunger certainly did.

Charlie began to sway with the ship as he walked across the deck. He was making his way up the steps to the helm, where Frids was barking commands at his crew. Lost in thought and faint with hunger, Charlie stepped into a glowing puddle of ooze and slipped, falling back down to the deck.

"Mind the sword!" Frids shouted at him.

Charlie looked up and saw the bears charging toward him, howling with delight as they prepared to stab him. He picked himself up quickly and grabbed the tiny arm of the closest attacker, heaving it with all his might and sending the teddy graham hurdling over the side railing. A loud squeal of pleasure came from the bear as it belly flopped into the waves below, bursting into a million pieces, lighting up the ship in its wake.

"A-10 was my first mate," Frids groaned. "He was the least helpful, but the most fun."

"Maybe try telling them not to kill me!" Charlie shouted.

"They won't kill you. They just like to stab a little."

"Any particular reason why?"

"They're universes. They're little balls of controlled chaos. It's what they do. Stop spoiling their fun and maybe let a few of them stab you so they feel better and get back to work."

"How about no?"

"Your loss. I've been stabbed about twenty times now, and it feels pretty good."

Charlie couldn't help but show his disdain. "Why am I not surprised?"

"Because you're a sour personality trapped in a 170-pound sweaty casing."

He considered arguing the point, but Frids wasn't wrong, so he just shrugged. He even started to smile, but then a sharp pain in his back forced a howl from his mouth. There was a sword sticking out of his lower back, and one of the glowing bears was waving happily at him. Charlie yanked the sword out, expecting to fall over from the pain and blood loss, but there was no blood.

"See," Frids said knowingly. "I told you it'd be ok." The unicorn laughed from the helm.

Charlie pressed his hand to the wound as the pain rapidly dissipated. He felt something soft and gooey on his fingers, and he raised them to take a look. The multicolored substance dripping from his fingers was more syrup than blood and smelled powerfully sweet.

"Good to know I can't be stabbed to death at least," he said.

"Just don't let them poke your eye," Frids warned, "because all you'll see is rainbows for several hours, and the distortion will make you want to vomit."

Charlie cringed. He loved rainbows, but he didn't want to be their source. Shaking the thought from his mind, he joined Frids at the helm and watched the bears race frantically across the deck. They seemed to be stabbing each other in order to get better positions from which to help sail the ship.

An explosion of light above the bow stopped the insanity. It came crashing down into the waves ahead of them. A cloud of dust poured out of the waves and rolled across the deck, knocking everything down. Charlie's eardrums were bursting with screams. He held his hands tight against his head until he realized he was the one screaming. Looking up, he could see Frids shouting orders to get back to work.

When he finally got his voice to work again, he said, "What the hell was that?"

"That's what we're trying to stop, Charlie. A universe and all life that existed within it just met its end. I'm sorry to say that the less of *you* there is in the universe, the rockier these waves will become. If we can't stop the anti-matter, it will eventually form a whirlpool that sucks all the waves into a black hole."

"Where did it come from? I didn't even see a speck of light from where it fell."

"You may only see a vast expanse of darkness above, but the whole of the multiverse still exists in the darkness. What you see is what I've highlighted to help me focus on my work to save the multiverse."

Dueling desires flooded Charlie's mind. There was an escape route from this insanity a mere few feet away. He may have been depressed and suicidal in his old life, but at least he knew what to expect. If he went back, he could pick up where he left off. But the unknown had allure, too, not to mention the chance to save the multiverse. He felt something akin to uncontainable joy, something he hadn't felt since he was a child with an exuberant imagination. When left alone, Charlie used to plunge himself into extraordinary scenarios to save the world, save the princess, or save himself.

He had always imagined as a child that he would one day be relevant to the world and influential, admired by others for being different. The idea still appealed to him, enough so that he forced himself away from the thought of returning to his old life and strode into position beside Frids.

"So what is it we do now?"

"We show you something amazing. That bright speck up to the right is where you exist in a world filled with unicorns. We just need to moor ourselves to it and drag it down to the ship so we can enter."

Charlie looked dumbfounded. He had already accepted a lot in agreeing that this wasn't all a complete delusion—and of course Casey had helped when she verified the presence of the unicorn. But to grab a universe with a lasso so you could enter it seemed unnecessarily implausible. Then again he'd just watched a universe collapse into gravitational waves that were now rocking the boat violently.

"Is there not an easier way? Do you not have a spaceship or a wormhole that we can just enter another universe through without all of this? It seems a little dramatic and unnecessary."

"Charlie."

"Yes."

"How much do you know about interdimensional planes?"

"Not much," he shrugged.

"Intergalactic travel?"

Charlie sensed he had hit a nerve.

"How about interstellar travel, or even just interplanetary travel?"

"I know we get around the planets with a rocket."

"Oh, a rocket," Frids said. "The most basic form of exiting a planet's atmosphere while existing in a Type Zero civilization. That must make you an expert in transuniversal travel even though I know for a fact that you're not even one of the people who design and fly those meager rockets that can't even reach the speed of light in your universe."

"I was just asking a question," Charlie said.

"Well, next time think of a better one," Frids retorted.

Charlie sensed that Frids wasn't going to give him an actual answer to his question, so he decided to let it go.

"Just be ready to go when we get it on deck," Frids said. "This one looks a little angry and is going to be hard to tie down."

Although Frids's expression never changed—that goofy smile was perpetually scribbled on his cardboard face—Charlie could sense the unicorn's excitement building.

"You're enjoying this, aren't you?" he asked.

"My existence has gotten a little more interesting since you decided to try and end all life. So, yeah. It's been a terrifying kind of fun."

"Glad I could help."

Charlie saw the bears drop their swords on the deck as they took their positions at the mast and along the railings. A gigantic lasso was dangling from the crow's nest, waiting for a call to action. All of the magic Charlie had wished for as a child had finally replaced his mundane reality.

"Weigh anchor, F-11! Everybody else, let's bring it down," Frids shouted, sending the bears into a frenzy as they grabbed the lasso and began swinging it violently. When they released it into the black expanse overhead, it snagged the bright speck effortlessly. Charlie could tell they had practiced many times. Dozens of bears jumped down from the mast and tied the lasso to its base before trying to reel it in.

Frids locked the helm in place and shouted for Charlie to follow him. Charlie stopped thinking, stopped questioning, and joined the struggle to reel in the universe, which looked like a roaring bear in the sky. The whole crew was grunting and groaning as they pulled on the rope, a cloud of brilliant dust beginning to swirl around them as the rope chaffed paws and bodies, releasing specks of stardust.

Above them, the bright light of the new universe began to dim. As its legs came into view, its resistance seemed to dissipate. Maybe it recognized its brethren.

With one final tug, it fell onto the deck, colliding with the bears pulling it in and sending their crumbs flying. Charlie felt a moment of panic. Had they just destroyed a multitude of life with those scattered bits of bear?

His fears were only slightly eased as the bears tried to shove their bits and pieces back in place. It was futile. They cackled wildly, hurling pieces of themselves at their nearest compatriots and the chaos ensued once again.

"Is this what it's like every time you bring a universe down?" Charlie asked.

"No," Frids chuckled. "Usually it's a lot worse."

The madness continued as a food fight broke out. Small pieces of graham crackers were flying over the railing and bursting into light, a cascade of bears jumping into the waves after them. A torrent of lights shot into the sky as the bears returned to their distant origins, giggling in the night sky before blinking out of sight.

"Now it's much worse," Frids said as he watched his crew dwindle. Only a handful of bears had managed to piece themselves back together on the deck. "Much, much worse. But on we go."

Charlie and Frids started to head toward the bear that was lassoed and grumbling on the deck.

"You want to go first?" Frids asked.

Charlie began to back away, remembering his last experience with the cephalopod universe.

"Great!" Frids shouted. "Glad you're finally getting

on board with this."

Frids's hooves pushed against Charlie's back, nudging him within the snarling bear's reach and inside its gaping mouth.

"Be there in a minute, just need to tidy up here and make sure D-13 is going to be stable enough for reentry."

As Charlie plunged into darkness, he tried to unleash his anger on Frids, but it was too late. Nothing could stop the force that was sucking him deeper.

Thirteen

Charlie stared at his hand as his eyes adjusted to the light. There was a hard black outline encompassing his body and he felt dizzy. He was surrounded by wildflowers stretching into the distance, and he tried to make sense of their flat coloring and appearance. He grazed the petals with his fingers expecting them to be rigid but they were smooth and dewy. He looked up at the sun and noticed its clear outline and the cartoonish shape of its rays in the pale blue sky.

The oddness of everything entranced him. He sat on the grass and ran his fingers up and down the green blades, each one encased in a tight black outline. It looked exactly like a cel-shaded video game. As he had graduated from scrolling platform games, Charlie had become enthralled by the new 3-D worlds that more powerful gaming systems had been able to create. Now he felt as though he had been transported inside one of them.

"Nifty," he said, turning when he heard Frids shuffling through the flowers, spouting a plume of pollen from his snout. "I never imagined something like this could actually exist outside of a video game. Are we in an actual universe where this is reality?" he asked.

"Never is a construct of limitations based on the perceived abilities of a single point in time and space. I hope you realize we're beyond that now."

Charlie nodded his head as if he understood. He resisted his desire to reply or ask more questions and instead turned his attention to a ladybug that had found its way onto his hand. He slowly lifted his hand close to his face so he could study its remarkably bold colors.

His was filled with delight. He'd always been drawn to the secret world of video games, where the impossible was made possible by dreamers with the same desire he had to leave reality behind. Magic, monsters, and mischief supplanted the mundane misery of everyday existence. Along with them came a distinct set of rules that could allow the player to understand and excel at the game.

In a video game, you could instantly be a hero. With the pressing of a few buttons, you could change your life instantly. The universe created by software held meaning and importance. Nowhere else could you find glory and adoration in such a quick fashion. But this wasn't exactly a video game, and he knew that with time, even the fantastic and extraordinary could become tedious and ordinary.

"I would imagine the me that lives here would find

this world just as commonplace as I find mine."

Frids sat beside Charlie, shaking his snout to get rid of the last remnants of pollen that were stuck to his face. "Intrigue isn't inherent. It fades at an equal rate to one's desire for comfort."

"I never found comfort."

"No. Your brain never let you find a sustainable degree of happiness. Skulking in the shadows of fear and anger doesn't preclude you from being able to feel comfort. It leads you directly to the confines in which you feel most comfortable. Of all the versions of you I've visited, each has decidedly chosen to spend more time locked inside their home, avoidant of all things existing outside save for a few people and a few indulgences. You may not have been happy, but you certainly were comfortable. Even if that comfort was swathed in despair and self-hatred."

Charlie couldn't overcome the urge to argue. His whole identity was based on being perpetually uncomfortable, and given the fact that all the other versions of him throughout the multiverse felt the same way, he thought he had solid ground on which to make his case.

"If I'm so comfortable in my own ways—self-loathing, suicidal tendencies, and everything else—why do I keep succumbing to the desire to leave all of it behind? How does pain equate to a state of comfort when it is so painful that I constantly think of ways to end it?"

Frids sat quietly for a moment, kicking at the grass

and watching it bounce back into its rigid shape. "All human brains don't work the same, but some, like yours, turn the growing sense of comfort into a desire for non-existence. Leaving the inhospitable world provides a source of comfort that extends beyond the self."

"I feel like you're just pulling shit out of your ass right now."

Frids turned to look at his rear. He stood up and started walking around in a circle trying to get a better view. "Nope," he said, "everything is still coming out of my mouth."

"That's not what I..." Charlie muttered, "it's just an expression." Now he had to respond. "How do you expect me to believe that I'm comfortable in my depression and desire for death when I feel so unhappy in my own skin?" he said. "My brain actively works against me. My thoughts hate me. I feel pain from the moment I wake up until I can finally pass out at night. Any wonder and hope that enter my mind are engulfed by frustration and despair. There may be a few brief moments in which I manage to distract myself from the raging torrent of disaster that is my thought process, but I don't think that in any way can rightfully be described as comfort. It is the exact opposite of comfort."

Charlie stood up and began walking away from Frids. There was nothing to walk toward—no landmarks on the horizon—but he just kept moving his legs.

"I'm not trying to insinuate that you enjoy the feelings that you're forced to endure," Frids said, "only that they bring you more comfort than the struggle to fit into a society that you preemptively concluded you had been excluded from. The comfort of not having to conform was, and is, its own source of comfort. Even if you hate it."

Frids stayed a few feet behind Charlie, minding his hooves as he stepped through the grass, trying to avoid disturbing its odd beauty and the little creatures scattered amongst it.

"If this is your attempt at giving me a therapy session to convince me to stick around, please know you're fucking terrible at it."

"Well, if you can't be the best, be the best at being the worst."

Charlie turned around to glare at Frids, those unchanging teeth smiling up at him. The scribbled eyes looked even more childlike now with their enhanced color and thin black outlines. He thought about kicking him and making a run for it, escaping this interdimensional miscreant who assumed he understood Charlie's deepest frustrations. But when the silhouettes of two unicorns came surging across the pasture toward them, Charlie knew he wasn't going anywhere.

"You sure these things aren't going to just try and eat us?" he asked.

The two unicorns came sharply into view. One was a mountainous beast with a bright white body, a bright blue mane, and a green-and-gold horn. By its side galloped a miniature version, struggling to keep up. Its body was a soft tan color with a blond mane and a bright white horn.

"They look so much cooler than you," Charlie said, hoping to provoke Frids.

"I know, right?" Frids agreed.

Charlie could only shake his head in frustration at Frids's lack of self-awareness. He would have to find a better way to insult his irritatingly optimistic companion.

The unicorns halted a few feet from Charlie and Frids, a perfect circle of dust sweeping up from the ground and flowing past them. When Charlie tried to touch the cloud of dust, he was amused to see it immediately reverse course and fly back toward the unicorns without breaking its shape.

Shaking its head, the mountainous unicorn snarled, its mane flowing from side to side before it spoke. "My name is Berkley, and this is Cota, my daughter."

Charlie and Frids started to say hello but the miniature Cota cut them off.

"We shall bask in the blood and dine on the flesh of the human!"

"Oh, goddammit," Charlie sighed.

"I misread this situation, Charlie. This one's on me." Frids stepped forward to address the two unicorns, but Berkley interrupted him.

"Easy, Cota. These two don't appear to be from the aggressive species," she said.

"Why take the risk?" Cota replied.

"Take the risk of what?" Charlie was too frustrated to be afraid. Being pissed off gave him enough courage to ignore the possibility of being gored to death by a unicorn's horn.

"The risk of you being a member of the aggressive species that is extinguishing our kind. Humans have plagued our existence these last centuries as they spoiled their land and now try to lay claim to ours. And although we may not view you as an impending threat, we would like to know why you're trespassing on our territory. Only those of an Equus class are allowed to walk these pastures. And while you are clearly in violation, human, we are not so sure about your friend." She focused her gaze on Frids, his cardboard body looking even more ridiculous in contrast to the magnificence of the real thing.

"First, he and I aren't friends—," Charlie said.

"We're best friends," Frids cut him off before he could continue.

Unable to stop the frustrated groan escaping his lips, Charlie glared at Frids for a moment before continuing. "Second, we didn't intend to trespass."

"Not intending does not excuse the actual act of doing so," Cota smirked, pleased with her cleverness.

"She's got a point, Charlie," Frids said. "You're bad at explaining things. Maybe you should work on that."

"I didn't...I wasn't..." Charlie seethed as he stumbled over his words. His impatience with the situation was becoming uncontrollable. The brief stint of being psychoanalyzed by an interdimensional being had left his emotions raw. "You brought us here, you busted ass piece of trash cardboard with a toilet paper horn. Why don't you take a moment to explain our situation since your persistent insistence that I live is the reason why we're here?"

"Persistent instintent. Pertisent incendence. That's a tongue twister," Frids said with amusement.

"You don't have a tongue!"

Frids continued to try and say the words correctly. "Persistent insistence. Ha! Got it."

"Congratu-fucking-lations!" Charlie shouted, his voice ringing throughout the pasture around them.

An awkward silence formed as the unicorns stared at them. They waited patiently for one of the two to explain their presence, but as the pause grew longer, Cota could no longer contain herself.

"The two of you have babbled on but said nothing of significance. Explain yourselves or you will be extinguished. Our patience and civility cannot be lent to a species that doesn't respect our existence indefinitely." She leaned forward, her horn glistening in the sunlight as it neared Charlie's chest.

Berkley did not try to stop her daughter this time as she stepped closer to Frids, her eyes peering at him as her horn grazed his cardboard neck.

Frids turned to Charlie as Berkley's horn scraped across him. "I think she likes me."

"We are here by mistake," Charlie said. "This one's

mistake to be more precise." He tried to punch Frids but his hand missed and hit Berkley's horn. Its rigid edges cut open his skin and perfectly shaped teardrops of blood trickled down to the grass below. "And, although it may not excuse it, our intent was not to trespass or bring harm. We apologize in full and would happily vacate your pasture if you would kindly show us to a path that will exit this place."

"Psst...Charlie. You forgot the part where I'm an interdimensional being and we're on a quest—."

"Not a quest," Charlie said, shaking his head.

"Yes, it is a quest. And it's to save you from killing yourself and destroying the entire multiverse." Frids paused, waiting for Charlie to jump in with some sort of disagreement. As the pause grew longer, Frids decided to try and speak louder, turning to the unicorns. "We're on a quest—."

"We heard you," Berkley said, shaking her head, her long mane flowing in the breeze. "We heard you because we are right in front of you."

"High Council?" Cota asked.

"Indeed. Follow us or those drops of blood staining the grass will turn into a river pouring forth from your body." Berkley no longer seemed to want to ease Cota's murderous inclinations but rather seemed to want to help her act on them.

The two turned and walked away from Charlie and Frids. Their tails flowed like their manes, swaying effortlessly with their movements.

Frids turned to examine his rear—he didn't have a tail—and his head drooped in disappointment. "Why didn't I get one of those?"

"Because you're not special and no one likes you."

Charlie didn't wait for a response, leaving Frids to continue staring at his rear while he moved forward, following the lead of Berkley and Cota.

Fourteen

THE HIKE THROUGH THE pasture felt endless. Even after hours of walking, the view never seemed to change; the mountains were still just as distant on the horizon, the grass still stretched infinitely to Charlie's sides. It was peaceful but highly unnerving.

As he marched, Charlie lost himself in thought, something he had little time to do since he encountered Frids. He wanted to think about Casey. He tried to hear her and see her. She was the only relief he'd ever found while trapped inside the Escher maze of his mind. Only her blend of blunt honesty and subtle compassion could guide him out of his labyrinthine thoughts. Without her, he always fell deeper into depression.

"I just want you to be able to endure happiness when it comes around. You fight against it at every chance and succumb to the same weakening thoughts of fear and anger."

Charlie closed his eyes and groaned softly. He had inadvertently arrived at his last conversation with her, the one before she left their relationship. The one that left the scattered remains of the Millennium Falcon spread across his floor.

"A fleeting moment doesn't change the overall story. It's a distraction. It tries to imply that something different may happen when the inevitable is lurking, waiting for a brief moment of contentment to make its entrance once again."

He remembered how her eyes grew sullen. Her movements and expressions were so familiar to him. She was his guiding compass toward happiness when his mind didn't get in the way.

"That moment is still worth enjoying. It shows that you can have something other than what you default to."

Charlie's heart was racing now. There was no avoiding or changing what had happened in the past.

"What's to enjoy Casey? I live an unwanted life with nothing of significance to say otherwise. Am I supposed to assume that because I smile from time to time all my problems are a mere figment of my imagination, that my pain can somehow be adjusted by thinking positively and hoping for the best? I want hope. I want joy. I want peace. All of these things I've tried to have and want to enjoy, but they are just outside of my grasp. They taunt me as they pass by speeding away at the first sign of contentment."

"It's not that you smile, but what you're smiling for. The world that most of us live in is paved with defeat and unwanted memories, but that doesn't mean we can't try. You've seen my struggles. You see how hard it's been for

me to fight through depression. I'm not someone who has no idea what you're going through. I've been down on my knees before, begging for my brain to let me live in peace. I fought through my desires to walk away from life and found people who could give me the strength to live and see the joy beyond the pain. Charlie, there is help out there. You just have to be willing to accept it."

"I've tried! I've tried therapy. I've tried medications. I've tried giving it my all. Trying means nothing when the outcomes never change. Ignoring the inevitable solution doesn't make you a hero, it makes you an idiot."

Charlie tried to halt the memory. He tried to think of anything else—late night video games, excessive amounts of homemade nachos on movie night, and hours of poring over detailed instructions to build their next monument in the Lego-verse. But he was stuck and unable to stop the painful memory.

"So seeing more for our relationship, hoping for a future of happiness with meaning, that makes me an idiot?"

He should have hugged her. He should have apologized and begged for her to help him. But he didn't. He just kept talking.

"I've seen you eye the door and I know you've felt the draw to leave this relationship. Don't try to convince me that you've ever felt any long-term desire to stand by my side. Happiness never has meaning in a relationship when you have one foot out the door. You ask if you're an idiot for seeing more for our relationship. I ask whether or

not you ever even wanted this relationship, or if you just stayed because you felt sorry for me and thought you could be my savior by leading me down your own self-aggrandizing path."

Memories can hurt even more than the moment that's remembered. The act of reflection and understanding can create a much greater sense of regret long after the emotion of the moment is peeled away. Her tears trickled through his mind, her silence felt like a knife. He was the cause of her pain, and he'd done nothing to stop her from leaving.

"Charlie!"

Frids's voice cut through his painful thoughts. He blinked and felt a few tears tumble down his cheeks, wiping them away before he would have to explain.

"What?"

"Is this a little anticlimactic? I feel like it is, but I'd like to get your opinion on the matter."

Before them was a nondescript barn. It had drab brown boards framing a vaulted roof bearing a crest of a unicorn horn surrounded by stars. Charlie began walking around it, looking for something a little more distinctive. The wood was rotting in some spots and cracked in others. This was the inner sanctum of the High Council of the unicorns' special universe? It was completely unpleasing to the eyes and the mind, and so contrary to the promise of those beautiful wildflowers and the majestic grassy landscape, not to mention the two glorious unicorns.

"Human person!" Berkley shouted. "Can you come back here? We don't want to chase you if you're thinking about running."

Cota chimed in. "If you do, I will skewer you with my horn and drag you back as your blood drips to the ground."

Charlie stared at Cota. The minuscule horse's apparent thirst for carnage was unsettling, but for the moment the frustration on her mother's face suggested there was no imminent threat to his life. He looked at Frids, who was absorbed by the unicorns' tails again. His mouth was chomping at the air around their backsides, trying to snag hold of either tail so he could inspect it more closely.

"Sorry," Charlie said. "I was just looking around to see where the rest was."

"The rest of what?" Berkley stared at him, puzzled by the statement.

"The building."

"The building is right here."

"But it seems so...unimpressive. I imagined the high council of a majestic being would heighten our sense of power and wonderment."

"That's a rather careless thought," Berkley said with a powerful shake of her head that sent a ripple down her back all the way to her tail. Frids, who had just managed to latch onto Berkley's tail, was launched up into the air and tossed back and forth. "Why should this not be our place of residence for the High Council?"

"People where I'm from build massive and opulent structures for those deemed to be worthy enough to sit atop a 'High Council,'" Charlie said.

"What relevance would a building of great stature have in comparison to the work done inside it?"

"I suppose it would make that work appear more important." Charlie didn't have the strength for a more robust argument.

"Appearing important is not the same as being important. The desire to occupy every aspect of the natural surroundings is what spoiled the human territory to begin with. Lack of forethought is found in every gaudy structure built from a perceived notion of necessity. Abandoning reason for luxury is a cost paid in droves. We will not pay the same price as your species, no matter how hard they try to make us. They may not value their continued existence, but we do."

"Your continued existence isn't important either," Cota sniped while walking closer to Charlie, nudging him toward the front of the barn, pressing the sharp tip of her horn against him as if she were seeing how deep she could go before getting in trouble.

"Let's not put ideas in his head," Frids said, finally joining the conversation after being tossed to the ground by Berkley's tail. "I've worked hard to keep this one in existence."

"Well, that's a weird way to phrase a response," a high-pitched voice said. All four of them looked at the entrance of the barn, where a unicorn as big as Berkley stood tall. Its body was covered in fine hair the color of lavender, its mane a dark blue shade that absorbed light. "Why do you say things so weirdly? And why are you made of such a flimsy substance?"

"These two were found wandering our pastures," Berkley said, unphased by the arrival of this new unicorn, a creature that had Charlie worried.

"Oh, well that's not good. Why didn't you just let Cota kill them?"

"I offered multiple times," Cota whined. "They've broken the line of demarcation."

"I'm sure you did, you murder-obsessed deviant." The unicorn laughed, or at least Charlie assumed it was a laugh. It made unpleasant little grunts while sucking in gulps of air. "That's why you're not allowed to go out on your own yet."

"Hi, I'm Frids."

"Nice to meet you, Frids. I'm Stanza, and I'm a little put off by your presence."

"Is that a compliment?" Frids asked.

"It's a statement."

"Can I take it as a compliment?" Frids said. "This one," he pointed at Charlie, "just stares at me dumbfounded most of the time." Charlie tried his best to look aloof rather than bewildered.

"That's an odd request but I have no objection to how you think."

"Can I object to how ridiculous this situation is becoming?" Charlie cut in, frustrated with the meandering conversation. "Also, I thought we were here to meet the high council. Are there more of you in there?"

"Now that," Stanza said, "feels a little insulting." He stared at Charlie with dark unblinking eyes as he inched closer. "And no, there are no more members. They were all killed in battle by your kind." Stanza sniffed at Charlie, saying, "You smell different from the others we've known."

"So it's not just me," Frids said, coming up to sniff at Charlie like Stanza did. It wasn't easy with a cardboard nose.

"Can we please just have a real fucking conversation before I lose my goddamn mind!" Charlie shouted before he could stop himself. His lack of restraint was met with Cota's horn, which lurched toward him, piercing his side and lifting him clear off the ground. Before he passed out from the pain, he saw glistening teardrops of blood trickling down Cota's horn to the meticulously shaped blades of grass below. It was beautiful.

Fifteen

Everything was blissfully calm. The shadows Charlie found himself drifting through felt pleasantly warm against his skin. He could tell his eyes were open, but he couldn't see anything.

He took a few steps to test the terrain below his feet. If this was an afterlife, he would need to keep his wits about him.

The ground didn't yield any clues as to where he was. It was flat and had no bumps or cracks. It didn't remind him of hiking trails or highways.

Maybe it was an alien space deck, like the ones he'd seen in movies. The thought made him laugh. If anyone could create the perfect floor, level to the nanometer, it would be aliens. He had craved interaction with such beings as a child, yearned to walk with them through their impossibly constructed spaceships, learning the secrets of the universe while leaving behind his own drab world.

The promise of life so advanced and prosperous had

once given him hope. But then he grew up. He began to study logic and reason. He let go of fanciful notions of UFOs and beings beyond comprehension. Skepticism had superseded imagination, that is, until he met Frids.

But was Frids even real? Now that Charlie wasn't in the presence of the cardboard unicorn, he began to doubt that it had ever even existed. Maybe he'd actually jumped off the mountain and landed in a snowdrift, and he was still alive and delirious, having hallucinations loosely based on fragments from his past.

He remembered something about a unicorn. He didn't want to think about it but a vision of the living room in his childhood home came to him.

His father, a man of tall stature but a short temper, was storming around the room, yelling at him. The sound was muffled, and Charlie struggled to hear the words.

He tried to look his father in the eyes but he couldn't. Eye contact always made him feel uncomfortable. Then he heard what his father was saying.

"Why can you not just be normal? Of all the hopes I have for your brothers and sister, I'm stuck with the knowledge that you are careening your way into nothing but stupidity."

Charlie remembered this sort of tirade. He had often done something to displease his father. When he failed to succeed in sports, failed to get good grades in class, or failed to be considered normal by anyone who met him, it was made clear by his father that he had failed his family as well.

"How hard can it be? I did it. Your mom did it. Everyone in your damn school does it. How can you not go one day without carrying that damn thing around with you? How can you not go one day without embarrassing this family?"

His father pointed at Charlie's hands. Charlie looked down and saw he was clutching something tightly in his fingers. It was a little crumpled, but he recognized it. His fingers trembled as his father raged at him, but there was no way he was letting go of his beloved cardboard unicorn.

"That thing has made you the laughingstock of your school not to mention the neighborhood."

His mother's voice was distant. *"Do you know how many times I've been forced to explain how I'm not a bad parent because of your problem? You have to start growing up, Charlie."*

"I'm not a problem." Charlie heard his own voice, though it sounded higher pitched than he remembered. *"He's my friend and keeps me company."*

"Your friend?" his father shouted. *"Children are friends. A dog can be a friend. Even a demonic cat can sometimes be a friend. That is a piece of trash."*

"He is my friend!" Charlie shouted. A slight sense of weightlessness came over him as he relived the memory, unable to escape. His vision became blurry with tears.

The stomping of his mother's heels surrounded him. Charlie knew she was storming toward him and felt his body tense, eyes closed, as he awaited the discipline they thought he required. He braced for the impact but instead felt a violent tug on his arms. He opened his eyes and saw his mother trying to grab the unicorn out of his hands.

As Charlie watched his only childhood friend being yanked from his fingers, he cried out. His father pushed him to the ground. "*Rip it up and let's be done with this,*" he ordered, turning his back to Charlie.

Charlie watched helplessly as his mother tore apart his unicorn, his companion, the only thing that seemed to accept that he was different. His cries were ignored. He still held a piece of his friend that had ripped off. He heard the scurrying sounds of his siblings behind him. They may have picked on him at times, but they too had felt the wrath of their parents. It was something they all shared. Something they had tried to bond with him over as they all got older, but he was too stubborn to respond.

With his friend in tatters on the floor, Charlie wanted to leave, to escape to some other existence, some other life. There had to be something better than this. But there was no escape, of course.

His mother carried pieces of his friend to the trash bin. When he heard the lid shut, Charlie knew his friend was gone, along with the only sense of security he had to help him face the outside world. The scrap he had left in his hand could never be reassembled into a unicorn.

The memory faded around him, and he was alone in

the dark.

Sixteen

AN OBNOXIOUS RINGING IN Charlie's ears reminded him that he needed to get up. He reached instinctively for his side as the pain flooded back. The image of his body being pierced by an aggressive unicorn was hard to forget.

The tear in his shirt was evidence of his encounter with Cota, but the wound had healed, and now there was only a scar. He grumbled as he sat up, disturbed by his vision. He saw Frids sitting nearby, having an idle conversation with Stanza and Berkley.

Charlie looked around for any sign of his assailant, but Cota was nowhere to be seen. That didn't mean the creature wasn't lurking in the shadows, hoping to sneak up and attack him, but the lack of blood pouring out of his side gave him a small sense of relief and hope.

"Are you sure your theory is correct?" Charlie heard Stanza ask in his high-pitched voice. "He seems quite scrawny and easily made porous to affect anything on such a large scale."

"A simple and poor design, yes. But that's what makes them so vulnerable and damaging. They die so easily, and they engrain themselves in their surroundings to find better and more parasitic ways to infect the flow of life."

"On that, we can agree." Stanza's gaze fell upon Charlie. "It would appear our other guest has returned from his slumber."

Frids stared at Charlie with his unwavering smile. His expression did not suit the tone of the conversation. He was beginning to wonder if Frids was enjoying the pain Charlie was being subjected to.

"I'm not sure what you are talking about, but I can only assume a simple 'go fuck yourselves' is in order."

"Not at all, but I can understand where your frustration is coming from." Stanza walked over to Charlie. His manner was unthreatening, but Charlie wasn't letting his guard down. "Cota has been sent back into the fields, so you have no need to fear another incident."

"You won't mind if I don't take your word for that, will you?"

"Cota may have been the one who injured you Charlie, but Stanza was the one who healed you." Frids hopped up on the table beside him, poking Charlie with his bent horn in an attempt to scoot him over so they could share the space.

Charlie wasn't inclined to move, but he gave way, allowing Frids his desired position. The memory of his childhood friend was fresh in his mind, and he felt a strong urge to connect with the interdimensional be-ing. He had no desire to spill his memory out into the world, though.

"I'd be interested to know how you intend to follow through with the information this entity has given you. While it may be your choice, we also have a role to play in the outcome." Stanza's tone was calm but steadfast. Charlie would not be able to avoid explaining his in-tentions.

"I suppose it's safe to assume he told you that the fate of the entire multiverse is in my hands," Charlie said.

"It would be." Frids nuzzled his way between Char-lie's arm and body. "I felt it was an interesting conver-sation point to help keep them from dropping us out in the field while you were still healing."

"And interesting it was." Stanza sat down on his hindquarters, keeping his distance but remaining solely focused on Charlie. "The ramifications for one hu-man's outcome is not something we tend to concern ourselves with, considering the damage your species has done to our world. But I suppose we can't hold you ac-countable for something you haven't personally taken part in."

Berkley had been so quiet Charlie had nearly for-gotten she was there until she moved closer. "It seems unjust that so many forms of life should be subject to one creature's actions. I do not agree with the High Council."

Stanza didn't chastise her. Charlie could only assume that he was used to having multiple voices join a conversation when the council was at its height, that a counterpoint was welcome.

"I agree," Charlie said, his eyes fixed on Berkley. "I don't think my fate should tie into anyone else. The notion that the multiverse may be so easily centered on one individual life is a preposterous flaw, and I would like to disentangle any connection I have with everyone and everything."

"That's part of the problem, Charlie. We need you to be connected. We need you to be a part of the multiverse so the fabric doesn't tear and become weakened by your absence of matter." Frids jabbed his horn—that misshapen roll of toilet paper—into Charlie's side.

"Your friend makes a sound point." Stanza stood up and turned toward the open barn door. "No form of life is a truly isolated incident."

"We can be if we isolate ourselves from others."

"You may isolate yourself from others of your species, but you can't isolate yourself from all forms of life."

Charlie was becoming lost in the conversation as it turned into a philosophical debate with Stanza at the helm.

"Let us take the example of Cota as she exists in this current moment. She walks alone in the pasture, but she can surely not be considered separate from life. Every blade of grass beneath her feet, every insect and bird that flutters past—they each are sentient beings with their own perspective and they each are affected by her movement. She may walk apart from us, but she walks with life."

"I don't concede your point." Charlie wasn't intrigued or impressed by Stanza's injection of nature into the conversation. "I can neither interact with nor gauge the life that exists on such a small scale. And I doubt that my presence would be missed by the grass that reaches high toward the sun for sustenance only to be pressed back down by my boot. I suppose the pasture would appreciate the lack of my presence if it remained undisturbed to exist in the manner it has evolved."

"Your step may be a small hindrance to the grass, but it still rises back into place after you remove your foot. And I'm sure some sense of pain may be felt. But your foot may carry a bit of soil or a drop of water from a puddle, which can also make it stronger. We coexist to enhance the life of one another."

Charlie was usually inclined to ignore well-intended conversations about nature. "It's a nice subjective way of viewing our attachment to everything around us. But it remains subjective. You can't prove that my existence is in any way fruitful for other forms of life."

"No, I can't," Stanza said, coming so close that his horn rested lightly on Charlie's forehead.

Charlie remembered trying to write an essay about the play *Equus* when he was in college. It hadn't been easy. He had never understood the fascination with the equine form. But as he stared into Stanza's eyes, he started to feel like maybe there was something to it. Stanza had a hypnotic presence.

"Wisdom is lost on the feeble-minded," Berkley said impatiently. "I'm going to join Co—."

A blast erupted near the barn, followed by the neighing cries of unicorns and the pounding of hooves from all sides.

"It would appear our conversation is over." Stanza said as a herd of his brethren gathered in front of the barn. "I can only hope you change your mind, young human. We won't have long to live in this world, but that doesn't mean life is pointless. Life is worth fighting for no matter the inevitable outcome that lies in wait for us."

As Stanza charged away with the unicorns following him, he shouted, "Remember death and never fear the fate that lies before you!"

With those words, Charlie and Frids were left alone. The unicorns were heading toward the explosion. Charlie could only imagine the carnage that would ensue if the humans of this world got their hands on the weapons of mass destruction available in his universe.

"Should we help them?" he asked Frids. The sudden reminder of death sparked his sense of empathy.

"There's nothing we can do to help," Frids said, tapping on his chest.

"Don't you have some modicum of power that can reverse this and save them?"

"Charlie, I don't even have the power to save you. I

can only offer a solution for you to try and save yourself."

"This doesn't feel right."

"No. No, it doesn't. But we can still save many more lives by helping you than we can by you dying trying to help them." Frids pulled close to Charlie, tapping his chest to release the box with the red button, his hoof poised over top, ready to send them back to the interdimensional plane.

Charlie pushed the box back into Frids's chest with force, knocking the unicorn to the ground. "We stay and help. If you want me to find a way to live through life, help me help them."

"I don't think you understand what you're asking me to do."

"I don't think you understand just how adamant I am about this." Charlie would not yield his point and began walking toward the open air, his legs shaking as the ground trembled from explosions.

"Alright!" Frids shouted, raising his voice above the cries of war. "But if we do this, you listen to everything I say and stick right by my side. I can't have you dying in battle while I'm still trying to find a way to save the multiverse."

"Agreed."

Seventeen

CHARLIE HAD NEVER FELT an adrenaline rush so powerful as the one that overtook him when he stepped outside of the barn. Wide swaths of explosions continued to erupt as bombs peppered the fields surrounding them. As a cadre of multicolored unicorns strode past him, he looked to the sky to find the source of the destructive force.

A ship the size of a skyscraper floated in the air, its rugged construction conveying its function as an industrial machine of destruction. Black smoke billowed out of multiple ports, deepening the stains on the steep hull.

"I'm not sure what you want me to do here, Charlie," Frids said, bringing Charlie back to earth. There was panic in his voice.

"You're an interdimensional being that can lasso universes. You can think of some way for us to take on that ship," Charlie said sternly. He had been indifferent when Frids had dropped them into the last universe.

But he couldn't walk away and not try to help these creatures.

There was a wrenching noise from the ship as multiple mechanical arms began reaching out from its belly —their claw-like hands containing massive black cannon balls. As the talons spread out on each hand, a powerful force launched the bombs for another barrage.

The explosions knocked Charlie to the ground. He heard the terrified neighing of unicorns. He smelled fire.

"Make us a ship," he demanded.

"What's a ship going to do?" Frids said, his voice terse and his body shaking.

Charlie wasn't sure what he intended to do, or how he could stand up to such a destructive force. In the distance, Stanza's high pitch voice called out orders to take up battle stations. Staring out into the fields, Charlie could only see a few scattered sheds and no signs of weapons or armor. There seemed to be nothing with the power to take on the death machine above them.

"It's going to give them time. It's going to stand up to a bully that doesn't care about the damage it's causing. It's going to save this place from annihilation," Charlie said.

The wrenching noise returned as the mechanical arms emerged from the ship again. Another wave of bombs was about to be launched, and the unicorns were going to lose ground and be pinned in by the fire.

"Two seconds," Frids said. He stuck his nose in the ground and began digging a large circle around them with his bent horn.

"What are you doing?" Charlie said, impatiently. "Those bombs are about to drop and start killing unicorns."

"Every ship needs a landing pad, Charlie." As Frids completed the circle, he hopped outside of it. "I suggest you take a few steps back."

Charlie obliged and stepped out of the circle as a rush of air forced his eyes shut. As it subsided, he opened his eyes.

"This is the one you like, right?" Frids asked. "I remember seeing little versions of it in your apartment." Charlie nodded his head as he stared dumbfounded at an X-wing Starfighter resting on the ground.

Charlie could have stared at the X-wing for hours but these circumstances would not allow that luxury.

"Take up position in the astromech hold. I'll man the cockpit," Charlie said.

"What's an astromech?" Frids asked.

"It's a droid from the *Star Wars* movie. I will tell you all about it after we save this place. Just take your place behind the cockpit and try to find a way to connect with the systems of the X-wing. You'll be my eyes and ears to make sure this thing is operating functionally and not about to get blown out of the sky."

Charlie pulled himself up the small rungs on the side of the cockpit and lowered himself into the seat, grabbing hold of the helmet on top of the controls. It had red stripes on the top and the red emblems of the Rebellion on the sides. He was about to live out a boyhood dream as he donned the helmet and powered up the X-wing.

Explosions rang out around him as the X-wing lifted off the ground. Frids's voice rang through the comm system inside the helmet. "All systems functional. Get this thing off the ground and let's go attack some ass-holes, Charlie."

"Call me Red-5." His voice was stern as he pointed the nose of the craft at the sky and punched the engines, sending them flying up at a very high speed.

"Is that some kind of reference? If that's a reference, I don't get it because I don't know what you're refer-encing."

"Quite R-2. This is personal and I need to stay fo-cused," Charlie said, lowering the visor on the helmet, its soft orange tint helping to block out the bright sun shining through the smoke-filled air.

He set his sights on the mechanical arms at the base of the ship and spread the wings of the Starfighter into attack position. They split at the sides, reaching up and down, forming the majestic X figure that gave the Starfighter its moniker.

"We're going to take on those arms with the laser cannons first," Charlie called into the comm system. "We need to disarm this beast before we take on the main structure."

He banked the X-wing to his right, circling behind the airship before righting course and approaching it head on. Slowing the Starfighter, Charlie glanced down at the locking system on the screen. It blinked to life as the cannons lined up with the target and he let loose a barrage of firepower. A mechanical arm blasted free from the ship and hurdled toward the ground.

"Woo-hoo!" he shouted as he flew underneath the gaping underbelly of the airship.

"Great shot, kid!" Frids called out.

Charlie smiled as he locked on to another arm at the front of the ship and fired. He wasn't as lucky with this round. An arm was ripped off the ship, but it still clutched a bomb in its hand.

"Red-5," Frids's said.

"Talk to me, R-2," Charlie responded.

"I've got a broadcast transmission from the ship. Want to cuss out some bad guys before we finish destroying their ship?"

"Put 'em through."

"You're patched in. Let them know how we feel."

"Unknown airship," Charlie said. "You are flying in protected territory and you need to disengage before we blow your sorry asses out of the sky and let the unicorns seek justice on any who live through the crash."

"Unknown assailant," a garbled voice responded. "Break off your attack. Whoever the hell you are, this is not your business and you need to leave."

Charlie banked to his left and quickly righted the

X-wing as he faced the airship head on. He cut off his comm system before calling out to Frids, "Let's respond to their request." Lifting the nose of the Starfighter, Charlie flew up the side of the airship until he reached its viewing port and let a barrage of fire rain down on it. Little damage was done, but he assumed they would understand his intent.

"We've still got six more arms to take out, Charlie. Let's get back to work."

"Roger that." Charlie couldn't contain his smile. Flying an X-wing Starfighter was going exactly as he had always dreamed. "Let's finish th—."

A blast rocked the Starfighter. Charlie looked from side to side to see where the attack had come from. He had hoped the only weapons the airship had were the mechanical arms, but the blaster fire raining down on them proved otherwise.

"Full power to the deflector shields!" he screamed through the comm system.

"Deflector shields at maximum power!" Frids responded.

Charlie flung the ship from side to side, spinning it in mid-air to evade the firepower. "Evasive maneuvers are only going to get us so far. Keep those shields at maximum power and let me know—." Another blast rocked the Starfighter and Charlie momentarily lost control as the X-wing spun to the side.

He fought with the controls to regain balance and dived below the ship to take aim at another mechanical arm. Letting loose the laser cannons, Charlie managed to take out another arm and the bomb within its hand. Then the cannons on the underbelly of the ship began to fire at him.

"Red-5," Frids's said, his voice steady though Charlie could sense his concern growing. "I don't know how much longer we can handle this on our own."

"We just need a little more time," Charlie said. "Any idea what kind of defenses the unicorns have on the ground to combat this ship?"

"Whatever they have, I think we're about to see it," Frids said.

Before Charlie could respond, he saw a blinding bright light below. He stared at it in awe as a familiar shape emerged from it.

Eighteen

"It's so beautiful," Charlie murmured, nearly forgetting he was in the midst of battle, at least until laser bolts flew past the cockpit. The airship wasn't slowing down to take in the sight of magnificent creation rising from below.

It was a majestic beast of machinery.

"Mega-Corn," Charlie thought as he surveyed the massive mechanical unicorn. Its bright white exterior was covered with multicolored polka dots. Atop its glorious head shone a brilliant golden horn. Somewhere within its gigantic structure were the unicorns he had seen running into the field.

"It's amazing," Frids added.

"I'm diving down to get a closer look. See if there's any way we can patch into their comm system. They have to have one in such a large structure to talk to one another."

"On it."

Charlie banked hard toward the ground, the nose of

his X-wing pointed toward the unicorn as he rolled the Starship in an effort to avoid any blaster fire from the destructive airship above.

"Patched in. We got Stanza here with us," Frids said.

"Stanza!" Charlie cried out. He didn't think he would be this happy to know that the last member of the High Council was still alive.

"Good to see you've found a reason to live," Stanza said. "I'd love to chat with you more, but we have a pressing matter on our hands. Thank you for providing cover for us, but you might want to watch yourself up there."

Before Charlie could speak, the massive hooves of the Mega-Corn swung together. As they connected, a radiant beam shot from the golden horn. It hit the airship, rocking it violently.

"A few more shots like that and you'll have that thing blasted out of the air in no time!" Charlie screamed.

"A few more shots like that are going to take time," Stanza replied. "This machine takes several minutes to recharge. And they're about to respond with more bombs."

"Sounds like we have a part to still play in this skirmish," Frids cut in to the comm. "Charlie, let's go bust some bombs."

"On it." He punched the X-wing back toward the airship, setting his sights on the remaining mechanical arms. Laser bolts rained down but whoever was at the helm was aiming at the Mega-Corn, leaving him ample room to navigate the blaster fire. "Just like shooting womp rats," he whispered to himself.

"What's a womp rat?" Frids said, sounding annoyed. "If you're going to talk, can you at least talk to me?"

"It's a thing, a saying. Well, someone said it and I like it."

"That makes no sense."

"None of this makes sense. Why try to start sorting it out now?" Charlie said, locking onto a mechanical arm that had begun to lower from the airship. He blasted it to oblivion and tore a hole in the ship. A flurry of fire came right at him.

Charlie heard a massive rumble and then the X-wing was hurled wide. "Report!" Charlie called out.

"Left laser cannons disabled," Frids responded. "There's damage to the two wings on that side as well. Maneuverability is going to be cut drastically and the shields took a toll on that one."

"All right. We're going to test the proton torpedoes. Call out to Stanza in the Mega-Corn and see how long it's going to take for their next shot. I'm going to swing us above the ship and hope we can weaken it enough so the Mega-Corn's next blast will bring it down."

"Got it," Frids said, cutting the comm.

Steadying his breath, Charlie lifted the nose of the Starfighter and righted the X-wing. He prepared to launch the torpedoes.

The guidance system locked on to the ship's blaster cannons as they flew over it, and Charlie fired the torpedoes. Jagged holes opened up in the ship's side from the concussive force.

"Great shooting, Charlie. But it's time to get out of here. The Mega-Corn is about to fire, and—." Frids stopped talking as the airship exploded.

The blast shook the X-wing and it spun out of control. Charlie glimpsed the airship plunging to the ground as he fought to gain control of the X-wing. "Come on you no good piece of shit!" he shouted, trying to bank the Starfighter away from the falling airship.

He heard the boom before he saw the flames. The X-wing plunged toward the ground, nose first. Charlie's body flailed about, but he wasn't scared. He was happy. The darkness could take over.

"Wake up, Charlie!" Frids shouted.

The voice didn't make sense. It sounded too ethereal.

"No rest for the weary," Frids continued. "We need to get you out of this thing."

Charlie's head was ringing. He wasn't sure where Frids's voice was coming from. He had some aches and pains but nothing that felt catastrophic. He was still strapped into the cockpit.

"Maybe I could just sleep for a bit, if it's ok with you?" he said. He felt so tired.

Another loud round of blasts woke him up. He saw the wreckage of the airship he had helped bring down. The sudden realization of all the deaths that must've taken place on the ship began to weigh on him.

"They're all dead in there, aren't they?" he asked

Frids.

"War doesn't allow for happy endings, Charlie. Death is the only thing that comes with fighting."

"Where death may come for some, peace is allowed to prosper for others," Stanza said in a surprisingly steady and calm voice.

Charlie released the straps and pushed himself up and out of the cockpit. The X-wing was being circled by all the unicorns who had been inside the Mega-Corn, which towered above them like a magnificent beast of war.

"What you did was brave, and we thank you for it," Stanza continued, his mane blowing gently in the breeze. "We have nothing of value to offer you though, except our gratitude."

Charlie didn't know what to say. He had only once stood up to a bully in school, hitting him ferociously with a textbook before the kid could take another swing at the little girl he was tormenting. All he had received for his efforts then was a one-week suspension.

"Your gratitude is plenty," Frids responded for Charlie, who nodded in agreement.

"Then it is our gratitude we leave you with. We lost many friends at the start of this battle and it is time for us to bring them to rest."

"How many did you lose?" Charlie asked.

"The number is unclear. But the weight of the loss is just the same."

"I'm sorry we couldn't do more," Charlie said. He

had been so focused on the battle in the sky that he hadn't thought about what was happening to those on the ground. A sudden wave of sadness replaced the exuberance that had been coursing through his body.

"You did more than we could have asked."

Charlie nodded. Words couldn't convey what he wanted to express, so he let his silence honor those who were lost.

"It's time for us to leave, Charlie," Frids said. He was holding the small box in his hand, the red button underneath his hoof.

"Go in peace, and know you are always welcome in our pastures should your journey ever bring you back." Stanza turned and walked away from the wreckage of the X-wing, the other unicorns following him.

"You did a good thing here, Charlie," Frids offered, his voice calm, his scribbled eyes staring into Charlie's.

"Why doesn't it feel like it now?"

Frids didn't speak. Charlie assumed there was no good answer to the question. He grabbed hold of Frids as they dipped back into darkness.

Nineteen

Charlie and Frids plopped out of D-13's mouth onto the deck while the bear—the universe they had pulled out of the sky and tied to their ship—doubled over, coughing up the rainbow-colored gunk that accompanied their reentry. Watching the intergalactic vomit inch closer to his fingers, Charlie pushed himself to his knees and crawled across the deck to avoid having to touch it. In an unexpected bit of camaraderie, the other bears surrounded D-13 and lowered him to a resting position on the deck, then took turns patting his head gently.

It was heartwarming. After the senseless violence he had seen overtake the world he had left, this simple act of kindness nearly broke Charlie. He felt raw, weighed down by the harsh memory of his mother and father and his realization of the deaths he had caused.

Frids bounded past him, joining the other bears to check in on D-13, the creature that had joined their crew and quest. *Not a quest*, he said, cursing himself for using the word, even if only in his mind. A quest is a journey taken by willing participants in search of a greater glory or good. He had been neither willing nor convinced that what they were doing was good—fun at times, but not good. And the farther he was from Frids, the farther his thoughts drifted from all the unicorns. He felt himself sinking into frustration and despair.

Maybe everything he had done would prove worthless. The unicorns may have won the battle, but they were clearly losing the war. His heart pounded as he thought about asking Frids to take him back to the planet so he could continue fighting off any attacks while helping them rebuild and reclaim their civilization. But he was no warrior. He was just himself, a speck in the cosmos. Charlie thought back to his toy unicorn. *What could I have done with it by my side again?* he wondered.

Slinking away, Charlie headed across the deck and up toward the helm and Frids's quarters. The hatch leading back to home was tantalizing and would be easy to reach without the hassle of explaining his departure. If he stayed, Charlie knew he would have to divulge the memory of his childhood friend to Frids. He could handle the pain from that one memory, but he wasn't sure he could handle the fallout from a storm of previously suppressed memories.

After losing the toy unicorn to his parent's anger, Charlie had hoped he could will his friend back into existence so they could take on the world together. He'd held the last remnant of his friend—the feathery tail that had been torn off the unicorn's body—and imagined the adventures the two would share. He'd wished him to come back with all his might, but nothing happened.

He wondered where that tail was. Was it in a forgotten box with other broken bits of toys or had it been thrown away? He was lost in thought when he heard a familiar voice.

"Thinking of leaving?"

Charlie had waited too long to leave unnoticed. Frids was standing next to him. He had left the teddy grahams to finish taking care of their new recruit below decks, and now it was just the two of them, swaying with the gravitational waves that rocked the ship.

"Tired of almost feeling useless. Was thinking about going home to avoid it."

"We helped them, Charlie. You were useful and did a great thing that I didn't even ask you to do."

"To what end, though? The humans may have already come back with a bigger ship and blasted them into oblivion. I may have helped give them a reprieve, but I did nothing in changing the outcome of their future." Charlie wanted desperately to feel like his involvement was worth something, but his mind was unwilling to allow it now.

"We may not have been able to stop their war, Charlie. But we can still find purpose from the moment that may help you."

"If we could serve no greater purpose than that one moment there, then why did we go? I'm beginning to think you have no idea what you're doing." Charlie's desire to leave was seeping out.

"You wanted to see unicorns. I took you to see unicorns. The best information I had available about that universe didn't specify what was happening between species, just which species existed."

"Then where do you get this shitty information from?"

Frids sat silent for a moment, his stillness reminiscent of the toy Charlie had created. "Come with me."

"Not in the mood to go to another universe right now." Charlie said, watching Frids walk past and open the door to his cabin.

"No other universe in here, just a window into the existence I see." Frids didn't go inside but he left the door open and it creaked on its rusty hinges as the ship bobbed up and down, searching for the right momentum to swing itself shut.

Two options lay before Charlie, each pulling his attention equally. The hatch offered a sense of solace. No matter the pain of normal life, at least he knew what to expect. The door offered the unknown. What he had seen was terrifyingly unique but had not given him the sense of peace Frids promised.

"What's in there?" Charlie called out.

"Everything I know about life."

"Then what's out here?"

"Only what I thought you would want to see. All you have to do is walk through the door, Charlie."

He was bewildered. Every child dreams of seeing the magical world that lies behind the mysterious door. Charlie finally had the chance to see it now, but his sense of wonder had vanished. He stepped away from the open door and opened the hatch.

"I can't stop you, Charlie. I'm not a monster. All I can do is ask you to listen."

"And if I don't want to listen anymore?"

"Then I'll let you go. I'm not here to punish you, only to show that we can find a way for you to be happy. I thought that this, all of this would spark a desire for you to realize how fanciful the stretch of existence throughout the multiverse truly is. But if you don't want to listen, I'll stop talking. Every time one of you has asked to be left alone for good, I've complied. And each resorted to suicide."

The word hung heavy on Charlie's heart. He had been so sure of his decision to jump before, but now the muddled mess of information coursing through his mind from their misadventures was pulling him toward an acceptance of life. Nothing had eased the pain that pushed him toward the edge of that mountain peak, but the desire to see past it was holding him back. Frids was still there to keep him from jumping, and maybe Charlie was willing to postpone it.

"You've got two minutes."

"Two minutes will seem like an eternity to you where

I reside. I'll take a nanosecond."

"That doesn't make any sense, so how about you just walk in and I'll follow you."

"Want to hold my horn in case you get scared?"

"Shut up and just show me."

"As you wish," Frids replied before walking into the cabin. "Watch your step."

Charlie was already annoyed with his decision but managed to follow along, the creaking door swinging shut behind him. The room was devoid of light, and Charlie could see nothing. He waved his hand in front of his eyes but didn't even feel the air stirring against his face. He took a step back to feel for the door. It was gone.

He took another step. The floor beneath his feet was not made of wood. It didn't even feel like there *was* a floor.

"Frids?"

"Yeah."

"I thought you said you were going to show me what you know about life."

"Can you not see it?"

Charlie heard the soft tap of Frids's hooves, each tap setting off a bright spark until a fantastic array of lights surrounded him. Nebulas danced around his fingertips, spiral galaxies whirled around the room before erupting, and everywhere he looked, there was luminous life. Then he looked more closely, and he saw it was all circling a central, stationary point: a black hole radiating light around its outer rim. Everything abided by its authority. Everything except for Charlie and Frids.

"What is this?" Charlie asked.

Frids came toward him, stepping through the black hole, which sent a shivering quake through the mysterious cosmos.

"This is your universe as it rests now, patiently guiding itself through the confines of space and time that preceded it in the brief moment before the expansion of matter. All of it exists in the manner that it has for billions of years."

"If this is my universe..." Charlie's thought trailed off, his eyes searching the room.

Frids's hooves tapped again, and a spiral of brilliant light surrounded Charlie. His body was inside the black hole, and it was shaking him. It was trying to consume him, but its power was too weak.

"This is your galaxy. What you and your species have dubbed the Milky Way. Don't quite understand that name considering it doesn't comport with any observable fact known about the universe, but you all seem to enjoy it."

Charlie pushed his hand through the spiral, causing infinite specks of light to bound around the room. As they began to rush back into place, some of them were pulled to Charlie's body and began to rotate around him. They swirled around him at tremendous speeds before breaking free and returning to their place within the galaxy as a whole.

"I don't know how this is real," Charlie said.

"This is real because I don't exist within a galaxy or a universe. I exist solely in the interdimensional plane within the multiverse. I have access to all that is."

"How do you focus on any one thing when you have everything before you?" Charlie's question was as much for himself as it was for Frids.

"I had to learn when I started seeing a disturbing number of galaxies collapsing within universes, leading the universes to collapse into my plane of existence. I had to recalibrate the way I experienced the multiverse to see not just the individual structures but the infinitesimal animating force inside each and every form of life."

"What do I matter to all of this?" Charlie said as he pushed his way out of the black hole. He felt a sense of immediate relief. He waded through the galaxy's faint outermost spirals until he reached Frids.

"Existence isn't lived in a vacuum," Frids said. "Every form of life, sentient or not, pulls and affects all others around it. From minute to grandiose, everything has a specific place and role. This is what Stanza was trying to impart to you. Something within you is pulling the structure—built over trillions of years—apart. If I can't get you to recognize that your life matters, then all of this could crumble into nothingness."

"I want to go home," Charlie whispered.

"Charlie, please."

"I'm not...I'm not walking away from all of this. It's

just too much to take in at once. You say you had to get used to seeing the world from the entirety to the smallest forms of life. I'm used to seeing the stars of my galaxy as specks of illuminated dust in the night sky. You had to adjust your way of seeing things, and now so do I. I need normalcy. I need to know where I am before I go any further."

A quiet clap of Frids's hooves sparked a brilliant explosion. As the light faded, Charlie saw the grimy wood planks of the ship's deck. The floating universe that had been revolving around him had been scattered onto the walls of Frids's quarters. He stepped out of the room with Frids following behind and looked up at the expanse above them. The ship was gently swaying in the waves. The hatch was right in front of him.

"Let's go home," he said as he reached down and opened it.

Twenty

Charlie's head smacked the side of the bathtub as his body tumbled out of the backpack. Shocked by the sudden impact, he let out a gasp. Touching his hand to his head, he searched for an abrasion or blood. He felt a surge of water rushing from the backpack and hurriedly zipped it closed. Pushing himself up, he nearly slipped again, eyeing the tile surrounding the tub and its unforgiving immovability were his head to crack into it.

He'd had a fear of dying in a bathtub since he was a child, who had been forced to take baths. The threats—from the possibility of the water rising above his head when he was small to the prospect of slipping and cracking his head open on the faucet—had always made him exceedingly cautious. Right now both seemed ridiculous compared to smashing into the tub headfirst when being ejected from an interdimensional transport.

"How is this even real?" he mumbled to himself.

"All prospective realities are possible given they don't

break the laws of physics in their universe," Frids said.

Charlie winced as he ran his fingers through his hair, now feeling the lump forming on his head. He eased himself out of the tub and tried to shake out the ringing sound in his ears. His clothes were a little damp but not too bad. Charlie now noticed that his hands were no longer as colorful and crisply outlined as they had been in the unicorns' world. Everything looked normal again, and maybe it wasn't quite as appealing, but it was comfortingly familiar.

Frids was sitting on the vanity, inspecting himself in the mirror.

"What...?" Charlie started to say before he stopped himself, holding up one hand before Frids could answer. "On second thought, I don't care."

"All the better," Frids said. "Go ahead and get a change of clothes. You're starting to smell worse than you did before."

"Thanks for noticing, but I'm just going to sit down. You can deal with the smell in the same manner that I have to deal with you." Charlie stepped into his living room. The couch was beckoning to him and he headed toward it.

Frids was following him. "That last one was a little frustrating, I'll admit. I was thinking that a world of unicorns might spark something in you given your interest, but the end display of destruction could easily be viewed as disheartening. Although you did get to fly an X-wing and live out a childhood dream I managed to resurrect at an amazingly fast pace given the circumstances and pressure we were under."

Ignoring Frids, Charlie let his body fall into the cushions. The couch was not attractive, and he had purchased it because it was the cheapest he could find. But it wasn't uncomfortable, and it welcomed him into the familiar indentions his body had had made in its cushions over the years. He'd thought about getting something more colorful, something to liven up the interior of his home — Casey had begged him to do so as well—but he never had.

Frids sat quietly beside Charlie and stared out the window. "We can always stay here and walk around your world for a bit if you want to. It may be a little less dangerous than our experiences so far."

"You can remove the 'so far' from your statement. If I agree to go anywhere else, the chances of me dying—or watching someone or something else die—should be zero."

"I don't think it would express the same intent of my thought if I were to remove it. It would restrict the types of universes we can visit."

"That's the intent of my request."

"Request denied, Charlie." Frids pressed himself into the crevice between Charlie's arm and his body. "Chaos and calamity can be fun."

"What part of that sounds fun? Nothing we've seen has given me any reason to listen to you. In both worlds we've visited, we've experienced the murderous nature of creatures trying to subjugate life."

"All the more reason to try and enjoy what you have here. This world is far from perfect, but on a grand scale, progress and improvements have been made to enhance most forms of life."

Frids was infuriating, so Charlie resorted to ignoring him. He thought about taking a shower, but he felt too exhausted to move. He eyed the TV remote and wondered if watching a show he had already watched innumerable times would give him the blissful dullness he needed to let his mind recalibrate and prepare for what may come next. His hand began to inch closer to the remote when he noticed a note on the coffee table in front of him.

It was a piece of white paper folded in half with the words "Hey Dipshit" written on the outside. He recognized Casey's handwriting from all the notes they had exchanged. She believed love, in its longform version, could only be expressed when unencumbered by the restraints of technology. The cold and uncaring screen of an email or a text message had none of the warmth and affection of ink put on a page by a hand. She had told him she felt more connected to her thoughts when she wrote them out. He reluctantly obliged her request to do the same in response, but his lack of enthusiasm must have been obvious.

I should have been better, he thought before grabbing the note and opening it.

"First off, let me start by telling you what a piece of

shit you are for railing on me after I came over to check on you." Fair point, Charlie thought. "*With that said, grab your freaky cardboard friend and come over to my place. I want to talk about it with you, but on my terms so I don't have to walk twenty minutes home if you piss me off by deciding to turn into an insecure asshole again. P.S. Grab a pizza. I'll be hungry at some point and you owe me dinner.*"

"What does it say?"

Charlie sighed from exhaustion and the inevitable prospect of having to get off the couch. "She wants us to come over to her place and talk."

"Sounds lovely! Didn't want to say it if I didn't have to, but your place is rather boring. It could do you some good to sit in a home I can almost certainly assume is more interesting."

Charlie stifled the snarky remark racing toward his tongue. Frids was right, after all. Casey's place was covered with flyers and posters of bands and anime she loved along with photos she had taken during her travels around the country. She had dreams of living life to its fullest and loved to revel in the moments when she achieved that. His place lacked life. A few of his favorite lego sets were completed and displayed on shelves along with the meticulously constructed X-wing model , but there was little else. He chuckled to himself as he thought about buying some posters of unicorns to plaster over his walls.

Charlie's thoughts drifted back to the first time he

was invited into Casey's apartment and got the grand tour. He couldn't resist how the tour ended when he saw her undress and how she stood before him as he slowly traced her tattoos. At the center of her chest were the words *Memento Mori* with the image of a delicate black rose. She had taught herself to appreciate life while it lasted. Though Charlie didn't share her outlook—he couldn't convince himself to care about life for very long—he still admired her sense of purpose.

"Yes, lovely," Charlie murmured while pushing himself off the couch and onto his feet. His body groaned from the effort and begged him to let it lie in one spot for more than a few minutes. But he could hear her voice urging him forward.

"I'm taking a shower and changing before we go," he said. "Don't fuck anything up out here." Then he thought better of it. "You know what? Just get into the backpack now, Frids, so I don't have to worry about you, and I can enjoy a little peace and quiet before I get stabbed or threatened with mutilation by someone or something again."

"You can't hide from your problems, Charlie."

"I appreciate your admission of being a problem."

Frids paused, taking in the insult with a smile before continuing. "I think we're starting to become friends."

"Just get in the fucking backpack."

Twenty-One

The pizza warmed Charlie's cold hands on the walk to Casey's place. Its aroma was alluring, but he wasn't a fan of her preferred topping of black olives, green peppers, and sausage. It's not that the pizza didn't taste good, but why mess with the simple perfection of cheese and pepperoni?

He had been ridiculed—inexplicably—on more than one occasion for his culinary preferences. It made no sense, for example, that he would be mocked for liking vanilla ice cream best. It was delicious. Everyone knew it was delicious, which is why it was the most-purchased flavor in the world. The notion that people needed complicated flavors and toppings to make their ice cream special seemed like a desperate ploy to hide the fact that those people had lackluster and boring personalities.

Charlie's resentful musings helped pass the time as he walked, unconcerned with the passersby. City life no longer had the allure it once had, when he'd first moved here from the heartless suburb he'd grown up in. He stared at the sidewalk as he strode toward Casey's place. She had weird taste, but she wasn't boring at all, so maybe she was the exception to his rule.

Catching sight of the bus stop outside Casey's apartment, Charlie swerved ungracefully through the crowd, nearly slamming the pizza box into the back of a lady who had stopped to take a picture. He thought about saying something, but he didn't.

Letting his frustration pass, he pulled out his phone and texted Casey that he was outside. Simply walking up to her door, even though he was expected, seemed rude. Why knock on someone's door without warning when the consensus was that oftentimes no one was welcome into the safe space people had made for themselves?

"Just knock on the damn door when you're up here. And hurry up, I'm hungry", she replied.

Slipping his phone back into his pocket, Charlie did as he was instructed and headed into the lobby of her building. He had come to know the dull interior well with its various damp spots created by multiple dogs asserting their dominance.

He found himself at the elevator, waiting for its pleasant ding. He had opted to take the stairs his first time over, but even his preference for solitude was thwarted by the cavernous dark of the stairwell. A smattering of unfamiliar, slightly sinister sounds had made him far too uneasy. He had pushed himself to keep going, but he had decided to never take those stairs again.

As the elevator door opened, Charlie stepped inside. No one else was in the lobby and he was grateful to ride alone. It would take fifteen seconds to get to her floor and thirteen seconds to get to her door, and he closed his eyes and tried to slow his breathing. He needed to keep his emotions under control. He also needed to apologize while keeping a bit of emotional distance. Letting himself get overpowered by his feelings is what led to this particular search for forgiveness.

When Charlie got out of the elevator, he walked down the hall trying to avoid the creaks in the shoddy wooden boards that were in desperate need of being replaced. He tried to focus on possible flooring options so he wouldn't hesitate when he reached her door. It was an odd choice to distract himself but it worked.

As soon as his knuckles rapped on her metal door, Casey opened it.

"You took longer than I wanted."

"That's an odd statement considering your knowledge of what I've been dragged into."

"That still doesn't mean I don't get hungry, or that you can skip out of bringing me a free meal to make up for being an asshole."

There was a brief retort forming in Charlie's head, but he knew her frustration was warranted, so he kept his mouth shut.

"May I come in?"

"Pizza on the table, grab two beers from the fridge,

and leave that freaky fucking unicorn out of this until I say I'm ready." Her eyes trailed away from Charlie's as she peered over his shoulder at the backpack.

"He's been instructed to remain out of my space until you're ready."

Casey offered no sign of approval for his thoughtful instructions to Frids, but she backed away from the door and took a seat at her small table.

Charlie grabbed the beers and took his place across from her, waiting for her to start the conversation. He sat in silence while she devoured one slice and helped herself to another.

"You weren't supposed to hurt me again." The disgruntled tone he had expected was gone.

"My intent—," Charlie paused himself as he saw her eyes dart up from the pizza. He knew it was the wrong choice of words. It would be hard to play the intent card when he directly insulted her. "I'm sorry. I was...I mean, I don't know what I was. This whole situation has me questioning every ounce of sanity that I have left. Until you confirmed that this thing existed, I thought I was hallucinating."

"So that should excuse it?"

"It's not an excuse, it's an explanation. The two can be mutually exclusive. I didn't want to hurt you, but I couldn't control the exhaustion and insanity that was boiling up and I let it out in the wrong way and to the wrong person."

"Who would the right person have been?"

Charlie sat for a moment in silence, watching her eat the second slice. She was going more slowly now, taking sips of her beer between bites. He took a piece of pizza and cracked open his beer, trying to collect his thoughts.

"I don't know anymore."

"Poor answer, but I'll allow it."

"Your courtesy is greatly appreciated."

Casey gave a nod of acceptance as they both kept eating. Charlie could hear music playing softly in her room. He recognized the CD: it was one she had made when she was a teenager with anime and video game tracks. It eased her mind when she was troubled.

"Any good RPGs come out lately?"

"A few. I still find myself indulging in the retros, though."

"'90s retro or 2000s retro?"

"Little bit of both." The conversation was casual enough to smooth over the harm caused by their last encounter. "A couple weeks ago I switched it up and played through *Metal Gear Solid* in one night for a little excitement."

Charlie smiled before shouting, "Snake!"

Casey laughed and almost choked on her pizza. "Dumb ass," she muttered.

"You still think Revolver Ocelot is sexy?"

"Do dogs still piss in my lobby?"

Charlie nodded while taking another sip of his beer. He missed this.

"I remember when—."

"Not now." Casey's mood changed as she looked at the backpack by his feet. "I'm not ready to stroll down memory lane until we get this shit sorted out."

Charlie sighed and acquiesced. "I don't know where to start, but I can try to answer any questions."

"Sounds like a minimal effort to start, but fine enough. So why didn't you jump?"

Twenty-Two

Good questions can be hard to come by. Often it seems as though people are afraid to be direct, so they hide their inquisitions in circuitous or vague language.

Casey didn't fall into this trap. She knew the answers she wanted and went straight for them, no delicacy or indirection needed.

Charlie puffed on his vape as he searched for the right words. "It's hard to explain."

"Try harder."

"It's not that simple."

"Situations may be difficult but talking isn't."

Charlie was flustered. "I don't know why. I was ready to. I was happy too. My boots were off, I had eaten my sandwich—."

"You and that fucking sandwich."

"It's a great sandwich! I don't care what you say." He paused as she took another swig of beer and another bite of pizza. He could tell she was full but she was going to enjoy it until her stomach told her enough was enough. "Anyways, I was about to until Frids appeared and started shouting."

"Sounds unnerving."

"It threw my whole mind state off like a fucking mental I.E.D. was tripped."

"Odd choice in imagery, but I understand your point."

"I don't really know how to explain the rest. Everything I had planned was disrupted by Frids's arrival—and, frankly, his existence—that I didn't know what else to do but to try and figure it out."

"Do you still plan on killing yourself?"

Her questions left no room for subtlety.

"Living doesn't seem like the appropriate option, and I'm still considering alternative approaches at the moment." Charlie fell silent. He was grappling with a jumble of words in his mind, trying to piece them into a coherent thought. "Hope isn't as easy as some people seem to think."

"Then why indulge this freaky ass unicorn? You have the ability to end your life at any moment but you keep persisting. Maybe there's more of you that wants to live than you think."

Before Charlie could answer, a muffled scream erupted from his backpack, and the fabric started moving around frantically until the zipper finally gave way first to the prying snout of Frids and then his mouth: "She's making a good point, Charlie."

Charlie turned to Casey, his eyebrows raised in a

question that didn't need words. She waved her hand, yes, the unicorn could join their conversation. Charlie helped unzip the bag so Frids could get out, though he kept his hand on it just in case a surge of water was close behind.

Frids stumbled out of the bag and fell over on his back before righting himself. Charlie quickly zipped the bag up as he heard an eerie sloshing sound.

"What I was saying was—."

"We heard what you said," Casey snapped. Charlie could tell her nerves were frayed. "What I didn't hear was his answer to my question."

Frids and Casey turned to face Charlie. Their stares were discomfiting. It had occurred to him that this question needed an answer, but he had been hoping to avoid it.

"I wanted to see if Frids was right. I wanted to know if there was any real reason that I should live. I wanted to see what made me this way."

"And I have succeeded!" Frids's exclamation was ardent and proud. He trotted around the small kitchen and hopped up on the counter just above the table, nodding his head graciously as if accepting the applause of a nonexistent crowd.

"You're wrong." Casey's voice was soft and cold. She ignored the unicorn and kept her focus on Charlie as he averted his eyes to the limp piece of pizza on the plate before him. "You're still going to do it, aren't you?"

"No." Frids cut in before Charlie could answer. "I've

shown him the repercussions that would ensue from his destruction, and he has made a miraculous decision to keep the multiverse from imploding." Frids leaned over the counter and began poking Charlie with his bent horn to get him to agree. The rough feel of the cardboard scraping against his skin was anything but comforting.

"It's been fun but I'm still not sure that I should have to suffer so others get to exist." His voice was quiet and full of anguish. Charlie tried to swallow his emotions—they felt strong enough to set fire to the world—clenching his teeth to prevent even a scrap of pain from seeping out. "But I'm not closed off to the possibility that life can be made sustainably enjoyable again. Or, well, for the first time."

"We're friends now, and he likes hanging out with me in other worlds and in my dimension."

"Shut up," Casey snapped at Frids, her hand swinging out to knock him away.

"No touching!" Frids shouted as he shied away from her hand. "You don't want to experience my reality without being inoculated first."

"That sounds utterly disgusting." Casey's eyes narrowed in disgust.

"It does, but he has a point. I didn't listen and I still regret my decision."

"Unimportant to the moment. Charlie, I want to show you something," Casey said.

Charlie felt a growing desire to please her, so he

stayed quiet and waited for whatever she was going to show him. Frids was sitting in the pizza, oblivious to the tomato sauce that was seeping into his cardboard.

Casey reached into her pocket and pulled out a photo, unfolding it and sliding it over to Charlie. He could see himself, a younger version, smiling at school. He looked happy.

"What do you see?" Casey asked.

"Vague memories."

"Look closer."

"Can I look? I want to see." Frids tried to get close, but Casey held up her hand and halted his progress.

Charlie studied the photo. He was in third grade, sitting at a desk in his classroom. He could tell instantly because of the Starter Jacket and Super Mario Bros shirt underneath. It had been an epic year for him. He had finally gained access to the video games his siblings had gotten tired of, and they'd moved on to other interests, such as being popular and playing sports.

Charlie's eyes landed on the desk in the photo. There it was. His prize possession, his favorite childhood friend, and his consummate choice for show and tell.

"Where did you get this?" His eyes didn't leave the photograph, but he knew Casey was waiting for the question.

"It was in the box your parents sent to you after you tried to cut contact with them. While you were busy arguing over the phone with your father, I rummaged around the box and found a stack of old photos. I didn't know how long it would take you to get off the phone so I decided to wander down the memory lane that you never seemed to want to travel with me. You told me so little about your childhood that I had to find out about it on my own. I really liked this photo when I found it, so I took it."

"That's stealing."

"That's doing my due diligence. Our youth isn't smattered all over social media so I wanted to see if I could find any dirt on you before you could find any on me."

"That's troubling."

"That's accusatory."

"This is interesting," Frids cut in, shaking the pizza sauce off his hindquarters.

"You think this is relevant?" Charlie asked, ignoring Frids and the memory of his prized possession being taken away and torn apart.

"How the fuck could it not be, Charlie? The unicorn is right here, on my table, in my pizza, destroying my leftovers."

"Because I don't want it to be."

"This is exhilarating! Can someone tell me what we're talking about, though?" Frids couldn't contain his excitement as he began to bounce back and forth across the table, splashing pizza sauce in every direction.

"Tame your friend before I disassemble it," Casey seethed.

"Frids! Sit down. Casey, don't go there. I'd rather not

relive that."

"I'll sit down when I get to see the photo," Frids said before Casey could speak.

"Here." Charlie dropped the photo on the unicorn's snout.

Silence again. Charlie avoided Casey's gaze and began to wonder if he had let too much slip, worried she might ask for an explanation.

"This is helpful." Frids's excitement had waned as his curiosity gave way to understanding.

"How so?" Casey asked.

Charlie watched the two of them staring at the photo together.

"This is clearly why I'm in this form. It also reinforces my assessment that this version of Charlie is a little dim-witted considering he didn't pick up on this."

"Maybe some memories aren't worth retaining," he sniped.

"I agree with your assessment on his dim-wittedness. But, and let me state this as my prime source of discomfort, why the fuck do you exist?" Casey asked.

"I exist as a means of connecting the information stored in light traveling in between the multiverse, which is why I was able to pick up on the troubling nature of his continuing lack of existence."

"Do I even need to be here for this part of the conversation?" Charlie pleaded.

"Quiet, sweetie. Grownups are talking." Casey waved off his frustration and turned her attention to

Frids.

Charlie was equally annoyed and enchanted. It had been so long since he heard her use the word sweetie that his heart skipped and it took a moment for him to catch his breath.

"What do we do to make you go away?" she asked.

"I can't leave until he has guaranteed he will not commit suicide, preventing all of existence from plunging into oblivion. This version of Charlie, I feel, is my best opportunity at that. And his continued existence is proof of my assumption, seeing as all the others I visited killed themselves within the first few hours of seeing me. I thought we'd been over this."

"Just needed a little refresher. It's not a normal circumstance to have an interdimensional being threaten the destruction of the cosmos because your ex wanted to jump off a mountain."

"Would it help if I just jump off the balcony?" Charlie asked sarcastically, earning a glare from Casey.

"Maybe you should've done that before I decided to help. Because now, if you do, I will search the multiverse with this cardboard-wrapped piece of chaos and kill the rest of you in order to meet you in oblivion and then I'll proceed to kick your ass there."

"I like part of your plan," Frids remarked, peering at both of them.

No one moved or said anything.

"It's not safe," Charlie finally said, breaking the standoff. He reached for his backpack and pulled it up by one of the straps.

"And the destruction of the multiverse is?" she responded, her hand snatching the other strap of the backpack. The bag dangled precariously between them.

"I nearly got eaten by a giant squid, stabbed by a unicorn, then had to fight off an airship of death with an X-wing Starfighter."

"Wait!" Casey's eyes were wide open, her mouth slightly ajar. Charlie stared at the blue lipstick on her lips until she started to speak once again. "You got to fly an X-wing and you didn't start this conversation off with that?"

"It all happened so fast in the universe that I still don't think I've had time to admit whether or not it really happened."

"It did happen, Charlie. I was there," Frids said, seeming pleased to add his voice to the conversation again.

Casey's grip on the bag grew even tighter as she began to pull Charlie toward her. "If you got to fly an X-wing, then you sure as hell need to take me with you and get me in the cockpit of Star Fox's Arwing."

"It was fun at the start, but I wound up getting blown out of the sky," Charlie said, pulling on the backpack.

"Sounds like a good time. Quit bogarting all the adventures."

"You could lose your job if you're not here to work."

"You already got me fired, asshole." Casey yanked

hard on the backpack, pulling Charlie close enough to punch him in the gut, doubling him over.

"So it's settled," Frids exclaimed, hopping down from the table, smearing the carpet with remnants of pizza before placing his hooves on the backpack. "Let's go have some fun."

Charlie tried to protest, but her blow had driven the air from his lungs and he was unable to breathe, much less speak. He could only watch as Frids grabbed the zipper in his teeth and opened a path to the void, the darkness pulling them in and whisking them away.

Twenty-Three

CHARLIE CAUGHT SIGHT OF Casey as she released a terrifying war cry and slammed a glowing bear face-first into the wooden deck. There would be no mercy for any who dared break the bubble of Casey's safe space, even though those smiling creatures—each one of which embodied trillions of galaxies containing a multitude of life—sensed no danger until she began pummeling them.

"Could you control your rage for one second?" Frids shouted, hopping back and forth behind her, trying to sink his teeth into the tail of her shirt to drag her off a growing pile of bears struggling to get out of her reach.

"What the hell is this?" she shouted, her right hook connecting with the back of a bear that was trying to run away from her.

Charlie was conflicted. He wanted her rage subdued, but he was also surprisingly attracted to the aggression that had all those universes running in terror. He had always imagined that she had the spirit of a warrior trapped inside her, and now it was finally being let out.

"It's my home, and these are my friends." Frids's voice was muffled because he'd finally chomped down on her shirt and was pulling her away from the pile of glowing bears.

Casey's arm didn't stop swinging, but Frids managed to get her far enough away so her blows didn't land. As the battered bears limped away, Charlie went over to her, his arms up in surrender. He didn't want to wind up facedown on the deck.

"How about we put the rampage aside for one minute and find a better way for you to process where we are and what we're surrounded by?" he asked.

Though her teeth remained clenched, Charlie saw her eyes soften as she stopped struggling to free herself from Frids. Her arms remained raised, but she showed a willingness to listen, at least for a moment or two. That changed when a rather brave, yet idiotic, bear came charging toward them with a saber raised. Its cackling laugh rang throughout the interdimensional plane, and then it was cut short. Casey ripped the saber from its paws and stabbed it just above the eyes. A small hole appeared in the bear's head as Casey pulled out the sword, and they could see all the way through it to the horde of wounded bears that were staring at her.

Charlie turned to Casey and saw the saber gripped tightly in her hand. The shock of seeing her with a deadly weapon washed away the words he had prepared. His sudden attraction to her warrior spirit was replaced with fear. "What the fuck?"

"You have a problem with me protecting myself?"

"Nu-uh. Nope. Not allowed." Frids said, releasing her shirt and scooting behind Charlie, so he could scold Casey from a relatively safe position. "This is a no murder zone and you are in clear violation with your assassination attempt on a perfectly good universe."

"She didn't mean it."

"Didn't mean it? She grabbed the sword, rammed it through the bear's head, and twisted it around before pulling it out. I ask you, Charlie, how does any of that equate to her 'not meaning it'?"

"I would think the two of you would realize that talking about the person with a weapon as if she's not here is a bad option. And I didn't twist it. I removed it and it just happened to turn a few times on its exit."

"Well, isn't that special? Now she's threatening us." Frids plopped down on the deck in a huff, taking care to remain behind Charlie to avoid being stabbed.

"She's not threatening," Charlie said, though his explanation fell short when he noticed the saber was pointing in their direction. "Wait. Are you threatening us?"

Casey was silent for a moment before tossing the saber over the side of the boat. "Not yet. But I still reserve the right to reassess my decision based on the outcome of this situation."

"See," Charlie kicked Frids, motioning that it was safe for the unicorn to come out from behind him.

"She's only potentially threatening us at a future time. Much different than what you were thinking."

The three fell into a standoffish silence. The bears were taking turns shoving their paws through the hole in their comrade's head.

"No, no, no!" Frids shouted, rushing over to his crew. "Do not let your galaxies mingle with one another in there. I have a big enough mess on my hands as it is."

With Frids preoccupied saving galaxies and universes from colliding, Charlie cautiously made his way over to Casey, his hands raised once again. "Parley?"

"The sword's gone, dumbass. I'm not going to stab you."

"The thought never crossed my mind." He cautiously lowered his hands. "Never knew you'd be the one to stab anything."

"You don't know who I am anymore."

A sudden sense of shame overwhelmed Charlie. Since their breakup, he had not once checked in on her. When he saw her at the café, she was the one who expressed concern for him. The bullheadedness that kept him from wanting to know if she had moved on to another relationship also kept him from wanting to know anything about her life that didn't include him.

"I think it's fair to say I'm a shitty friend."

"More than fair."

"Fair enough."

"Super shitty."

"Adequately shitty, with an abundance of selfishness."

"Are you trying to somehow make yourself seem better by that statement?"

Charlie thought for a moment. While attempting to grab a sliver of self-respect, he had unintentionally admitted to his poorer traits. "There's no way to make shit seem pretty, is there?"

"Nope."

"Well, you want to mock my inability to be a normal functioning human while I give you a brief yet terrifying tour of Frids's home?"

"I'll allow it."

Eschewing the calamity on the deck and the mass of bears trying to put their paws through the hole, they went over to the railing. Charlie wanted to let her see the glowing lights deep within the sea. It was the only tranquil sight he had seen in this bizzarro realm.

"Here be the first stop in our tour through insanity."

Charlie's terrible impression of a pirate's voice drew Casey's attention far more than the mysterious lights did. "You're not going to do that again."

"It was just—."

"I'm afraid you thought I wasn't being serious with my previous statement, so I'll repeat, you're not going to do that voice again."

"Joy killer," Charlie mumbled as he gripped the railing and stared at the lights flickering beneath the waves. His fingers accidentally grazed hers. Casey didn't yank her hand away but slid it farther down the railing, away from his touch.

"So what is this?"

"Supposedly it's bioluminescent remnants of universes resting beneath gravitational waves, but I have no clue what that's supposed to mean. According to Frids, these waves are supposed to be tame, but as more and more of the other versions of me commit suicide, they get more turbulent and brighter as universes are yanked out from their position in the multiverse and drawn into this realm where they are destroyed." Turning to the expanse overhead, he continued his speech.

"Each speck of light is a different universe. Although there's a lot more out there now than there was before." He was surprised that so many bright new universes were visible. The new ones were cinnamon colored. "Last time I was here, there were just the honey-yellow ones. Frids said those were the few universes in which a version of me was still alive that had a chance of being saved."

Casey tried to count the number of universes that held Charlies but it was hard to keep track as the cinnamon ones became ever more dominant. "I don't understand."

"Neither do I. But the strength of the black hole forming in this realm, destroying all the life that gets sucked into it, makes it even harder."

"That's entirely disconcerting." Casey's look gave him the sense that she failed to comprehend the meaning or truth behind his statement. Her gaze lifted up toward the expanse above. "Why does it look like they're staring at me?"

"Because they are." Charlie turned her around, pointing at the mayhem on the deck. "Each one of these bears is a universe pulled from above us."

"Bullshit."

"True shit. I had to help bring one down and found myself being devoured and entering a world where unicorns existed. One stabbed me and another gave me an introductory philosophy speech."

"Goddamn unicorns. You know they're just disfigured horses with a pompous attitude?"

"Yeah, I know. Murderous little bastards," Charlie murmured, the image of Cato stabbing him flooding his thoughts. He laughed off the painful memory of being stabbed and tried to focus on the battle he'd helped them with. "They were the ones I tried to help, though."

"Why?" Casey turned to meet Charlie's eyes. Her lips formed a tight smile.

"They had no part in the humans who lived in that world destroying their lands, but the war was brought to the unicorn's home nonetheless. I didn't feel it was right and told Frids I wanted to do something about it."

"Which is when you got to fly an X-wing without me even though you knew I should've have been by your side flying."

"We couldn't both be Red-5. The call signs wouldn't have worked."

Casey glared at Charlie before punching him in the shoulder. "You know damn well my call sign would've been Red Leader. Wedge Antilles was a far superior pilot to Skywalker."

"Point conceded," Charlie said, rubbing his shoulder as the memory of how much Casey liked to punch him to prove a point came back.

"What was really cool though, was the Mega-Corn," Charlie said, smiling as her eyes widened. She took a deep breath.

"You have to take me there," she said.

"I don't know if Frids will take us back. He's intent on getting me to not commit suicide," Charlie said, slumping back on the railing as he stared up into sky. Casey let out a big sigh, clearly frustrated by the great adventure she'd missed.

"Why do they look like teddy grahams?" she asked.

"Everything seems to play off something from my childhood here."

"The cardboard unicorn," Casey added before he could continue.

"And honey teddy grahams. They were my favorite snack."

"Cinnamon is where it's at. Honey lacked flavor and was slightly depressing."

"Maybe for someone who needed an extra dose of personality, but for those of us with a more refined palate, honey was a delicacy."

"You think I have a dull personality?" Her fingers

started to form another fist, ready to swing at his shoulder.

Charlie stared into her eyes while searching for the right answer, hoping to avoid another dose of pain. "I retract my statement regarding personality."

"Damn right you do." She looked up at the glowing lights overhead. The glowing teddy grahams were shining in her eyes. "If you don't like cinnamon, why are there so many of those in the sky now."

"For you, I suppose. Maybe this place chooses who gets to see which universes when they arrive."

"What about the pirate ship?"

"What kid doesn't like pirates?"

With a slight nod of the head, Casey quietly responded, "True."

A cascade of screams broke out behind them. Swords were being drawn and Frids was running around trying to quell the battle that was about to ensue. It appeared that the bears had formed factions over who could take ownership of the hole and were now set to battle it out.

"How about we retreat to Frids's cabin for cover so as to not be stabbed by a sword?" Charlie said.

"I often choose the option to not be stabbed by a sword. I'll follow your lead, cabin boy."

The sly insult was left hanging in the air as Charlie ignored his impulse to respond, leading her up the steps to Frids's cabin, leaving the commotion behind.

Twenty-Four

THE WALLS OF THE cabin were pulsating. Scribbled across the wood panels was a multiverse in disarray. Nothing looked the same as before. Charlie recognized the buoyant yellow balls of light as the universes, but their glow was much more muted now, and many of them were crossed out with big red X's. He had a notion of what the X's might mean but was unwilling to put more thought into it to avoid the answer.

Charlie's fingers traced the images, feeling the waxy residue of crayons. As a child, he found it hard to stay within every line in his coloring books. It became easier as he got older. This drawing was the work of a kid who had yet to learn restraint.

He finally found a yellow universe that wasn't crossed out with a big red X. "This must be us," he murmured.

Another universe floated a few inches away. Charlie started to reach out to touch it but stopped when he saw a red line appear on top of it, slowly crossing it out with a big X. He felt a sudden pang as he was forced to reckon with the meaning - a different version of himself had just succeeded in what he had struggled to do.

He slammed his fist into the wall and screamed, "Fuck you! Why you? Why any of us?" It was not easy to confront the suicidal tendencies he shared with all the other versions of himself throughout the multiverse. The joy and ease he'd felt just moments ago was gone.

"Charlie," Casey whispered behind him. "Talk to me." Her tone had shifted with his. She'd spent enough time with him to understand his sudden mood shifts from ecstasy to depression.

His hand dropped to his side, and he leaned against the wall. He was so tired. "Ever since I can remember," he said, "I've wanted to die, and now I'm being told that if I die, I bring all of existence with me. It's not fair."

"How is this even possible?" she asked. "Explain it to me."

"The growing number of X's on these walls, they're all leading to the implosion of the multiverse if one version of myself doesn't stay alive. But no version of myself wants to stay alive because somehow my body contains the remnants of antimatter that seeks to destroy everything."

Saying it out loud, Charlie couldn't help but laugh. It was so utterly ridiculous that he could barely believe it.

"Why can't you exist?"

"None of us can. It's baked into who we are and I don't have a right to tell them they can't die. Life is torture, and if it's the same for them as it is for me, then I don't want to tell them to survive if I don't want to."

"I don't care about the others." Casey stepped over to Charlie, pulling him away from the wall. "I asked, why can't you exist?"

"You know my brain. You know what I go through. So why should I?"

"Because I want you to. Charlie, you deserve peace. You deserve the chance to feel happiness and not just pain. You deserve to be with people who can make you smile and show you that life can be good in those moments when everything doesn't turn to shit. You deserve to exist."

"I don't know how." His words held no malice or anger, only the fear of a child faced with a daunting task no one had prepared him for.

"I doubt this interdimensional dimwit does either. That's why I'm here." Casey pulled him close, wrapping her arms around him.

"Finally!" The two turned to find Frids coming into the cabin. Before the door shut, they could see the chaos behind him. He nudged his way between them, forcing them apart. "I've been waiting for you to join in. It's been my hope since seeking out the first Charlie that I could get a version of you, Casey, to get back with Charlie and help."

"Wait...I'm not...who said I agreed to get back with

him?" Casey stumbled over her words, worried she had suggested some sort of romantic inclination before.

"No, no. Your resolve has almost always been too strong to delve back into a relationship like this with him so resolutely depressing. No offense, Charlie."

"I believe I'll take some."

"I believe you should," Casey added.

"Well, if we're passing it around, I might as well take some since neither of you offered to help me keep those bears from battling with one another, possibly causing their galaxies to intersect, which could set off a massive extinction-level event throughout the far reaches of the multiverse. So now that we're all equally offended, let's talk about Charlie and his suicidal tendencies."

"What fun." Charlie moaned, turning his back on both of them so he could return to the disastrous view of crossed-off universes on the cabin's walls.

"Not much." Casey walked over and punched Charlie in the arm.

"What was that for?"

"Take a look around and pick something. Consider it a favor that my fist didn't land on your jaw or your balls. Although I still reserve the right to hit either, or both, at a later time and place."

"As much fun as it may be to torture Charlie," Frids said, "we need to focus. By my calculations, the antimatter residue in the multiverse is increasing exponentially, gaining more weight as they draw in other pieces, and worsening the vibrations within the gravitational waves."

Frids's point was emphasized by an enormous rolling wave that lifted the ship's stern high before dropping it down. They all lost their balance and Frids nearly tumbled off the table.

"Since I'm new here, can I ask a question?" The lack of response annoyed Casey, but she carried on as they stared blankly at her. "You said that if we stop one Charlie from killing himself it will keep the singularity from forming, but won't that just leave this place in the turmoil it's in if all but one Charlie die?"

A little miffed that he didn't think of the question, Charlie turned his attention to Frids. "She's got a point. Won't we all just die anyway now that things have gotten this bad?"

"No and no. And stop trying to find a way to kill yourself, Charlie. It's getting a little frustrating."

"Agreed," Casey added, punching her fist into Charlie's arm again.

"Would you stop that! It hurts."

"That one was for getting me fired."

"You did get her fired, Charlie. And you suck at apologies, so deal with your punishment."

"I don't suck at apologies."

"Yes, you do," Casey and Frids responded at the same time.

"Now," Frids said, looking at Casey, "I still have a chance of settling this place down so long as I have time. If we stop him from committing suicide, it will stop the flow of antimatter. Without a full particle being able to form, the singularity will be prevented, and I will have time to collect the residue that has found its way here and redistribute it to a universe that it won't have an effect on. Thus, it would save all of existence, making me a godlike hero that your species adores so much."

"I'm glad you haven't let this go to your head at all," Charlie sniped.

"Don't have a head. This is just a physical manifestation for you to feel more comfortable with."

"Does it matter that I don't feel comfortable with you at all?" Charlie grumbled.

"Not anymore." Casey grabbed Charlie by the arm, squeezing on the slowly forming bruise, dragging him away from the wall. "So where do we go now?"

Frids wasn't finished talking about himself. "That photo Casey showed us was intriguing. I took this form based on an assessment of data gleaned from the remnants of memories trapped in the residue that's made its way here, but I didn't know the story behind it. And I've met multiple versions of Charlie, but not one of them recognized me or even mentioned that cardboard doll."

"It wasn't a doll. It was an action figure."

"Keep telling yourself that, babe." Casey held up her hand just as Charlie was about to pounce. "That was a slip of the tongue in a confusing moment. Say anything and I punch you in the throat."

Backing away, Charlie tried to calm down. "Action

figures aren't dolls. They're active participants in competitive play."

"Wow. That sounds creepy." Frids's head tilted so he could get a good look at Charlie. "Doll or not—."

"Not!"

"Either way," Frids paused, expecting another interruption but Charlie kept quiet, "we might be able to get some sense of direction on how to stop the cycle if we find out why I look like this."

"Any thoughts?" Casey asked Charlie.

He was thinking about his parents scolding him before ripping apart his cardboard friend, but no way was he going to relive that moment out loud. He shrugged, no comment, as Casey stared meaningfully at him.

"Now would be the time to talk, Charlie." She leaned over and gently pulled him close enough to see the light shimmering in her eyes. The combination of blue and green gave them a dangerously alluring nature that made it hard to look away. "There's something's beneath the surface here. I've known you too long to think otherwise. I know when you're hiding something."

It was unnerving. If Charlie was good at anything, it was his ability to hide his feelings, to keep them locked behind a stone wall. But her gentle gaze left him wondering if maybe he had just been fooling himself. He had trapped so many emotions inside himself without ever addressing or dealing with them. His misinterpreted notion of Stoicism had led him to thinking that if he ignored his emotions he would master them. He knew this process was wrong, but he was too stubborn to admit it.

"They took him from me and killed him," he said very softly. It had been his first experience with the death of a loved one.

"What do you mean." She ran her fingers down his arm and clasped his hand in hers.

"I took him everywhere when I was a kid: to school, to the playground, to games. No one wanted to be my friend, but he wanted to be with me wherever I would go." He bit down hard on his inner lip to keep his composure. "I never bothered anybody with him. We always stayed to ourselves and left people alone. But it wasn't good enough for my parents. It made them look bad. It made them angry. It made them angry with me. I tried to please them. I could sometimes get them to smile when we performed plays and reenacted skits from TV shows, but it didn't compare to the shame they felt when other parents started laughing at me."

"What happened, Charlie?"

A single tear began tracing its way slowly down his cheek. He grabbed the vape from his pocket and inhaled so he didn't have to speak. He held the vapor in until he couldn't hold it any longer. Frids was leaning closer to him. Casey gripped his fingers in hers.

"They ripped him from my arms, then my mom started ripping him to pieces. My dad drug me up the stairs to lock me in my room, but first he slapped me over and over as I screamed for him to stop. My brothers and sister hid in their rooms, hoping to avoid his wrath. They tried to comfort me through my door after he left, but it didn't help. I never saw my unicorn again. All I was left with was a bit of the unicorn's tail I had managed to hold onto."

"Wow. That's depressing." Frids stared at Charlie for a moment before consulting the mind-bending map on the walls.

"What a wonderful assessment." Casey tried to kick Frids in his rear end but missed. "Charlie, do you want to take a turn and get out some frustration?"

Charlie considered the tantalizing prospect for a moment, but decided it wasn't worth it. "I would rather us both just forget this conversation." He wiped the last tears from his eyes, avoiding her gaze.

"You've got my vote," she said. "But I think the demon spawn has plans to put it to use."

Twenty-Five

FRIDS HAD USHERED THEM out of his cabin as he began furiously working, drawing lines connecting one universe to the next with an incoherent mumble. The more questions Casey and Charlie had begun to ask, the more insistent the unicorn had become that they depart.

They were out on the upper deck, resting against the railing and watching the few bears that remained wander aimlessly below. Charlie could feel a throbbing in his head from a lack of nicotine. He pulled out his vape and took a few quick drags to numb the pain. Releasing the vapor from his lungs, he saw it slowly drift down toward the waves.

"How is any of this capable of existing?" Casey asked.

"I don't know. You could ask our benevolent leader when he allows us back into the cabin, but I doubt he'll offer anything of substance to make you feel better about it."

"Thanks for the positivity."

"You're welcome. Some would say it's my best feature, but I think those people are just looking past my rugged adventurous side. Not to mention my stunningly superior emotional stability."

"Humility truly suits you."

"As do my clothes. Another fine quality most overlook. Wearing the appropriately sized apparel is quite sexy in my opinion."

"How charmingly simple of you."

Charlie enjoyed the back and forth with Casey; it was the first thing he had come to love about her. Finding someone he could talk to without having to restrain himself was remarkable. His jokes were much funnier when she was around. She understood all of them. She got the references and the nuances. It was so easy to be with her. Letting his guard down when he was around her was one of the best experiences he had known.

It was also one of the worst. Feeling free to say whatever he wanted was not always a good thing. He unleashed tirades of unimportant nonsense when he was frustrated. He complained about trivial nuisances. He nagged, whined, and criticized. He pushed her away and she began to push back and demand he respect her more. He knew she was right, but it was as if some sort of internal self-destruct code had been activated, and he couldn't find the button to reset it.

There was a multitude of better choices he could've made when they were together. He knew he was the one who caused their relationship to disintegrate, but at the time, he couldn't see beyond himself. He had been selfish. He was still selfish. But he didn't know if he could change it.

"I have no clue how any of this came to be. It all seems to be based around me. But which version of me? Frids says there are an infinite number of Charlies, so which one did Frids choose first, and why didn't the other Charlies recognize the connection between Frids and the unicorn we had as a kids?"

"Maybe, like you, the other Charlies did but were too pigheaded to say anything about it. You have a tendency to invest only in the emotions you want to express and shut down and stop talking when things get difficult." Casey gave no room for an argument or rebuttal. But, as if to prove her point, Charlie kept on talking.

"And how did Frids design it so that getting devoured by a teddy graham would make it possible to travel to other universes?" Charlie hoped Casey wouldn't make him address her "pig-headed" comment. He saw her shake her head in frustration, but she seemed willing to move on.

"Let's put a pin in the 'devoured by a teddy graham' part, because you said that way too casually as if it's not a horrific thing to imagine. So let's get back to the other versions of you. Have you met any? What are they like? Do they feel as regretful and shameful about making an arbitrary distinction between dolls and action figures?"

"They're not the sam—." Charlie stopped himself

from falling into the trap. There was a galactic divide between a doll and an action figure but he knew that no amount of discourse would enlighten her to the utter wrongness of her thought process on the matter. "No, I haven't met any other versions of myself. The two universes Frids has taken me to have been utter disasters nearly leading to my death, and not even at my own hands."

"Doesn't seem like Frids knows what they're doing?"

"We're on a rickety pirate ship drifting along gravitational waves and surrounded by monstrous teddy grahams. It's very safe to say they might be a psychopath."

"That might be a little harsh," Casey said. Charlie could tell she thought he was being a little harsh even though she likely agreed with him.

"Should we talk of the 'being devoured by a teddy graham' part? I don't know who or what chose that process as the way to enter different universes, but I guarantee you Frids had more control over it than I did."

Casey couldn't argue the point. "Then why follow them?"

Charlie almost had an answer to her question, but as he opened his mouth, it escaped into the air around them. *I have a reason. I must have had a reason*, he thought. He was both curious and befuddled.

"It's a simple question, Charlie."

"Simple questions don't always have simple answers. A person doesn't just ask 'why does the universe exist?'

and think that they'll receive a two-syllable response."

"You're avoiding the question and muddling the topic at hand."

"I'm trying to explain that it's a little deeper than you think."

"You're trying to give yourself an out."

"Well, maybe I fucking want out. Maybe I don't. Maybe I want to wake up in the mornings and feel like I can forget everything, and maybe I want to embrace everything. I don't know how to answer the question because there are too many factors to address that don't break down to the base models of conversational platitudes." Somehow she always got him talking. Whether for better or worse, she wouldn't let him sit quietly and brood.

"Right now," he continued, "I'm here because of you. The first time I was here was out of sheer curiosity. The second time was confusion and exhaustion. I don't know if there'll be a fourth or fifth. I don't know if I'll ever see you again after we get back to some semblance of reality. Shit, I don't even know if we'll survive whatever mess of a universe Frids tries to drag us into before we can go back home." Charlie thought he was finished, but the words just kept coming.

"All of that is to simply state that I don't know if I want to be alive," he said. "But if I'm going to be alive, I want my life to have some sense of meaning and purpose. As much as I want to save all of existence, I can't just continue to carry on if my life is going to be the same as it's always been. I'm angry and frustrated all the time. I'm a shell of a functioning person and a pain in the ass to be around. The reason I'm here is to see if there is anything more to live for, or some way for me to contribute to a world that I've sucked so much joy from."

Silence. It spread across the ship's upper and lower decks. The bears had scurried away a long time ago, early in his tirade. They were alone. He couldn't read Casey's expression. He felt a sinking moment of guilt—he wondered if he'd said something hurtful—and prepared himself for her response.

"Thank you for being honest," she whispered, grabbing his hand and pulling him close. She rested her head on his shoulder. "I don't want you to die, but I'm not going to tell you that you can't. I just want you to be sure that it's the right thing to do before you do it, because I won't be able to pull you back from the ledge after you leap."

Charlie leaned into the hug, a vibrating sensation tingling throughout his body. It had been too long since he had held another person's hand, let alone embrace them. A person forgets how needed human contact is after such a long drought.

"Thank you. I—."

His response was cut short by the unicorn's frantic shout as Frids burst out of the cabin door.

"Who's ready to do some mind-bending travel throughout the multiverse?"

Twenty-Six

THE WALLS OF THE cabin were entirely covered with indecipherable marks and scribbles. It looked like the work of a madman. Messy, multicolored lines arched over and through the universes. None of it made sense.

"I see we've gone insane," Charlie said, walking along the walls, trying to glean some sort of pattern, anything that would ease his growing concern that Frids had prepared a haphazard plan.

"Only if by insane you mean clever and stunning," Frids chimed in. He was sitting on the table, looking pleased with himself.

"No. I'm pretty sure he means it in the literal sense." Casey looked like she was frozen in place. She hadn't moved since shutting the door.

"I don't think the two of you appreciate the sheer brilliance of my intentions."

"I think you think we have a clue what any of these lines mean," Charlie stopped to look at each universe, some of which had been circled in blue. He wanted to go to all of them. The anticipation of adventure was building with each scribbled universe he passed. "Maybe take a second to say why anything you've done here is relevant and worthwhile."

He saw Casey's hand moving back toward the door. He could tell she was worried. If she thought there was any chance of finding normalcy outside the cabin, she would have already left.

Frids hopped down to the floorboards with an exasperated sigh. "These lines are a new perspective, one I've missed since I started trying to help the different versions of you. Even though my theory was correct with the anti-matter residue, I was unsure of how to stop it from garnering enough control that it would make you kill yourself. Now I have a clear direction to follow by tracing the link between your toy – a smaller and less impressive version of me – and how it subdued the reaction of the anti-matter residue. And if you weren't so depressing and glum, I might have found this sooner."

"Again, offense taken."

"Offense allowed." Casey let go of the door and came over to the wall. "Carry on."

"Case in point," Frids nodded toward Casey. "Her persistent questions about why you turned into the curmudgeon you are has been entirely missing from my analysis. I never once knew why I came to you as a cardboard unicorn even though I'd scanned your residue-tainted memories, but she was able to drag it forth from the recesses of your mind."

"Her insulting me and, in turn, allowing you to insult me doesn't sound like a solid method of stopping antimatter residue from ripping its way out of my brain to coalesce into a destroyer of the multiverse here. Don't want to be the downer of the group—."

"You most certainly are," Casey interrupted. "You're like the long drive home from a vacation. You're like the flat tire you find out you have when you're already running late for work."

"I think you've made your point," Charlie broke in.

"Wait. One more. You're like a bill from the doctor."

"I don't get that one," Charlie said, scrunching his face as he tried to piece together her meaning.

"Nobody likes getting a bill from the doctor, Charlie. It's always depressing."

"She has a valid point," Frids added, his janky smile staring at Charlie.

"First, fuck you both. Second, the point I was trying to make is that just talking to her isn't going to make me not want to commit suicide. If you haven't noticed, I've been talking to her for years and I still wanted to throw myself off the ledge of a mountain."

"I've always been attracted to your compliments. That's what made me want to slide in bed with you and ponder the depths of disheartened sex."

"Totally uncalled for!" Charlie shouted. "I know for a fact you had a good time at least some of the time."

"Point conceded, but you might not want to take

that as a glowing endorsement of your abilities," she offered with a smile.

"This!" Frids shouted. "This interplay is what I needed to spark your desire to at least give me time to piece together this puzzle and give you a reason to live."

"Sounds wonderful, but again, how does any of this resolve the issue of the antimatter?" Charlie's question was pointed, his level of irritation rising as a resolution seemed to be getting farther and farther away from where Frids was leading them.

"The antimatter issue can only be resolved by finding the triggering mechanism that ignited it." Frids began moving around the room, tapping his horn on different blue circles, igniting a brilliant glow. "Were it strong enough to drag the multiverse into oblivion, it would have done so eons ago. Somehow, while sheltering in your body, the residue formed a bond with you that allowed it to influence you. Your suicide would let it depart from your form to reconnect with the rest of itself in this interdimensional plane."

"His parents ripping the real version of you up." Casey was walking along the walls, studying the glowing blue circles. "So if these universes you have circled are the ones in which he's still alive, the Charlie's that live there probably still has an intact unicorn."

"Precisely!"

"But you said yourself that you've seen versions of me that had a good life, so they wouldn't have had that happen, yet they've still killed themselves."

"They didn't need to." Frids gently caught Charlie's hand in his mouth and dragged him to the center of the room. Releasing his hand, Frids clapped his hooves together, and the brilliant multiverse came to life around them. Casey gasped with fright and lunged toward Charlie to steady herself. The universes were floating all around them, connected by a blue line. A decrepit pirate ship was drifting about, too. "This line traces how just the one instance of your unicorn being ripped up and lost had a ripple effect. Other versions of you became even more dependent on their unicorn to stabilize the draw that was released, leading their parents to act in the same manner as yours."

"So you're saying my bad childhood was the instigator of the destruction of everything?" The prospect was demoralizing and slightly torturous to think of.

"Someone's feeling pretty shitty right now, huh?" Casey smiled at him, trying to break the tension building in his mind.

Frids seemed oblivious to the comments and simply carried on. "Just a few instances were needed to free enough of the antimatter so that it could begin its dangerous work. And yes, your horrible childhood was enough to set in motion the impending destruction of the multiverse. These lines trace the connection between the various versions of you in each universe. Even if a version of you has a good life in one universe, it can be dragged down by the weight of another version of you succumbing to the anti-matter."

Charlie stared at Frids, a blank expression etched across his face. "Yay."

"So his parents were assholes. A lot of people grow up feeling that way."

"It's not about his parents, but what they did that unlocked the catastrophe. His smaller, dare I say less special, version of me was his key to happiness when he was younger."

"Look Mary Poppins, finding happy thoughts doesn't drive away the terrifying thoughts in my brain." Charlie was growing visibly irritated. "Realizing my parents hurt me was Therapy 101 and didn't do shit to make me feel better. I knew it when I was a kid. I knew it when I grew up. That's why I stopped talking to them unless absolutely necessary. And, fun fact, I still want to kill myself."

Charlie raised his hand toward the pirate ship. He leaned forward to poke it and felt a massive vibration under his feet that swayed all three of them back and forth, their rocking perfectly synchronized with the miniature ship's.

"You're missing the point," Frids said. "And stop trying to destroy my home. Now, this isn't about your parents. It's about you and what you knew you needed, even when you were a child. Your unicorn friend kept you safe. You probably didn't know why, but he kept you happy and gave you the ability to function. When your parents ripped him away from you, you lost that ability."

"Point being?"

"We need to find your unicorn." Casey stepped beside Frids, her disappointment replaced by a look of determination. She shuddered as her body passed through an expansive black hole. Her fingers curled from the vibration of her body. "What the hell is this?"

"It's a scale model of the multiverse in relation to the areas we have left to explore to keep Charlie alive. Don't break it."

Charlie's frustration was obvious. "So you think I, at my age, just need a cardboard unicorn to feel better. Again, must I state how trivial and pathetic that sounds? You could send me back to my apartment now and I could cobble one together, and I guarantee you it would make no difference whatsoever."

"You're right on one account." Frids motioned for Charlie to follow him. The unicorn hopped up to tap a universe with an X across it. "You even tried that in this universe but to no avail. You downed a bottle of antidepressants with a bottle of whiskey and never woke up."

"Maybe I was just a little tired." Charlie's voice sounded flat and indifferent.

"Fun joke, but let's hear him out," Casey said, emphasizing her point with another punch to Charlie's arm.

"You don't need *any* unicorn. You need *the* unicorn. The one you created as a child to specifically help you deal with this problem. In some transient way, your childhood mind must've recognized the problem and found a solution to cope with it."

"So how do we find it? His parents ripped it up years ago. It must've decomposed or be covered under years of rubbish in a landfill."

"In your universe, yes. But for those Charlies who needed this unicorn to protect them from the antimatter, the possibility of one existing at least mostly intact is highly probable."

"Yeah, but if we take it away from another version of me, then aren't you just dooming that one to commit suicide?"

"That's where this 'haphazard' plan comes in. We go to a universe you've already committed suicide in and find it there, leaving the other Charlies to maintain some sense of preservation." Frids plodded around the room, tapping his bent horn against various points of interest, and sparking a brilliant light from each potential source. "Each one of these universes has at least a minimal amount of your unicorn remaining in it. The brighter the glow the more there is. And if we can piece together a full unicorn, I believe you can dampen the effects of the residue, helping to keep you alive, while also giving the other remaining Charlies a better potential chance at living as well."

"One plugged hole in a sinking boat doesn't keep the crew from drowning."

"No. But plugging one hole allows the crew to move on to others to try and stop the boat from sinking altogether."

"Fuck it. I'm in." Casey was ready for action. She waded through the universes, letting her body spin around as she scattered light all about the room. Then her hand accidentally grazed the pirate ship. The sudden shock of impact let out a terrifying scream from the teddy grahams roaming the deck outside the cabin door. "That one's on me. My bad."

Charlie wasn't optimistic, but he couldn't help but feel stirred by Casey's exuberance. "I still think this sounds stupid," he said, "but I'll play along for now." He followed Frids and Casey out of the cabin to the deck to quell the screams of the teddy grahams and find their next universe in the expanse above the ship.

Twenty-Seven

"No. Uh-uh. Nope." Casey was completely unwilling to go along with the notion of wrangling a teddy graham universe from the sky so that it could devour them. Charlie had just explained the means of travel through the multiverse, and her enthusiasm for their mission had dwindled instantly. "I'm not being eaten by a snack made for children."

"And how do you propose we travel between the realms of each universe?" Frids said. "We have to break the bonds of my dimension and find our way towards the planet you two reside on. It's not exactly easy." The unicorn trotted around her in a huff, disgruntled by her opposition to his plan.

"You were the one who went all-in on this a few minutes ago," Charlie said. "If you're going to throw a wrench in the plans, you better have an alternative option." He was enjoying her discomfort. He'd been unsettled by her insistence that he travel around to piece together a lost toy, and now was slightly indulging in her discomfort.

"How is it not possible to simply travel somewhere in a spaceship? This is literally the best place to have a spaceship and be futuristicy and whatnot."

"I'm sorry, but you seem confused." Frids plopped down in front of her. "Are you familiar with interplanetary travel?"

"No."

"Interstellar or intergalactic?"

"No. But..."

"No buts. Spaceships may be suitable for that type of basic travel. But we're inhabiting a completely different frame of the cosmos. I have calibrated our expedition perfectly to the point where we just have to step into the mouth of a bear to arrive at our destination. And besides, I don't like spaceships and I don't want to use one."

"But I like spaceships," Casey insisted.

"The lady makes a solid case," Charlie said.

Frids rubbed his head with his hooves, before holding them up in surrender. "Fine." Clapping his hooves, a gigantic cardboard spaceship fell to the deck from the sky, rocking the boat and causing Charlie and Casey to lose their balance. "Just know that you've made me do something I don't like just to appease you, and not because it's as effective or efficient as my means of transporting us."

"Quit your—."

"It's her!" Casey's shout interrupted the squabble.

"Who's her?" Charlie yelled as Casey ran past him to their new means of transport.

"The Rockette!" she shouted, opening the door of the spaceship and disappearing inside it. Her head poked out of a porthole in the side. "I built her when I was a kid to travel throughout the galaxy." She disappeared again, and Charlie heard the thumping sound of her footsteps.

"What did you do?" Charlie looked down at Frids, who was making his way to the spaceship.

"I gave her the spaceship she always wanted, even if I think they're dumb."

Before Charlie could ask more, Frids disappeared into the spaceship. The flimsy cardboard door was splattered with stickers of skulls and crossbones—an early indicator from Casey's youth of who she would grow up to be. There was a scenic route to be had for entering the ship, and Charlie felt the urge to take it. He walked around the cylindrical ship, avoiding the sharp fins at the base, taking in the various drawings of multicolored stars streaking across the cardboard. A plethora of youthful stickers were interspersed with the drawings: teenage mutant ninja turtles, animaniacs, and a random assortment of monsters. This was the fort of a badass, and he never even knew it existed.

Casey had never mentioned the spaceship. She clearly wasn't ashamed of it, but in all their long, detailed conversations, she had never once talked about her Rockette. Before he could analyze her lack of communication further, he was pelted by a barrage of wadded-up construction paper.

"Dude, get in here. I can finally fly this thing and you're holding up the launch sequence!"

There was no denying her glee. Charlie didn't even try to hurl the discarded pieces of paper back at her. He opened the door and stepped in, finding himself under the watchful eye of movie posters and somehow even more stickers. He ran his fingers along the walls as he made his way up a sharp incline to the cockpit. The walls stood firm to the touch. They were assembled from construction paper, serving the purpose of its designated name far better than it did in the reality he had been used to.

The stairwell began to wind upwards and Charlie took a look out of the porthole. The teddy graham crew were circling the Rockette in awe, waving their paws goodbye. He was going to wave back, but voices were coming from the cockpit and the ship was about to take off.

"Boosters?" Casey asked.

"Check," Frids replied diligently, tapping scribbled buttons on the panel in front of his seat.

"Life support?"

"Check."

"Mentos and diet soda?"

"Optimal levels attained in ten seconds."

"Charlie, if you're back there, you better strap in before this sets off!"

Charlie got into the cockpit. He was surrounded by the crazed imagination of a child. Small stuffed animals, dolls, and plastic dinosaurs were strewn about the control panels.

"Get used to the feeling of staring up at the stars and get in your seat," Casey barked.

"Optimal levels in five seconds," Frids chimed in.

Charlie saw an empty seat behind Casey. It was a child's school desk, complete with an uncomfortably small chair, and he didn't know how he'd get his knees under it. He grabbed a handful of dinosaurs and squeezed them in his hand as he painfully maneuvered his body into the seat. Once he was seated, he put the dinosaurs back, hoping Casey wouldn't get upset that they had been moved.

"I take it you know how to fly this thing?" Charlie asked.

"If it flies as it did in my imagination, I'll get us there and back without a single scratch on your pretty face."

"Should've told you." Frids traded glances with Casey and Charlie. "Just because you imagined flying when you were a kid doesn't mean you know what you're doing."

"Wait. What?" Casey's question went unanswered as an explosive force lifted the rocket from the deck of the ship and sent them soaring into the expanse above.

The cockpit rattled, bouncing their bodies back and forth as they fought to maintain upright positions in their chairs.

"Get a hold of this thing, DUI Joe!" Charlie shouted as his head continued to slam against the construction paper covered with dials and readings.

"Your face isn't that pretty anyways. Maybe a few bumps and bruises will give it character." Casey grinned as she looked back and saw Charlie bouncing around in his miniature seat. She tapped a few buttons on the walls and scrolled her fingers up a line of switches, stabilizing the interior of the cabin. "Ha! I knew she would fly true to form."

"Impressive." Frids unstrapped himself from the chair to inspect her work as the ship sailed smoothly toward the glowing bears hanging precariously in the expanse above them. "You really thought this through."

Charlie wanted to offer his congratulations as well, but the growing smile of a cinnamon-flavored teddy graham was growing ever dominant in the cockpit window. "Should we be worried about that?"

"Did you enter the navigational coordinates?" Casey flipped through the construction paper at her panel until she reached the navigation log.

"Entered and set," Frids replied as he walked out of the cockpit and down into the stairwell. "I'm going to head into my crew cabin to reconstruct the multiverse in there so we have a traveling view of our destination."

"Roger that. Use the comm system if you need anything."

"Aye, aye, Captain." With that, Frids disappeared into the construction paper.

"Nope. Can't happen. I walked around this ship before I came in and—."

"Charlie. It's the ship I dreamed up and built when I was a child. I can create and do anything in here. A crew cabin for Frids. Sleeping quarters for us. A fully stocked kitchen with all the sugary candies we got yelled at for eating too much of when we were young. I can do it all in here."

"Why didn't you ever tell me about this? It's amazing."

Casey's glee vanished. She turned her focus back to the panel in front of her, scrolling through the logs and dials she had created.

"How often do you like to talk about the moment you realized your creativity peaked?"

It was an odd question, but its intent was clear. There's an unrecognizable moment in life when a person reaches the height of their potential. When it's happening, everything seems to be headed along a trajectory that goes far higher than you already are. It's only after you've fallen that you realize you've already gone as high as you are ever going to go. For Charlie, it was the death of his unicorn. For Casey, it may have been her last flight as a child in her Rockette.

"You don't know that you've peaked. You're one of the strangest and most creative people I've ever met."

"I work—worked—at a café as a waitress. Just because you love and indulge in others' creativity doesn't mean you have any. I haven't done anything nearly as meaningful since I built this."

"Until now." Charlie unstrapped himself from the school desk and walked over to the panel beside hers, taking Frids's place.

The light shining outside the cockpit window was getting stronger, highlighting the intricate work Casey had done as a child. It was the magnificent creation of an unbridled mind free from the constraints of physics and reality. He lost himself in her youthful imagination until he felt a gentle tap on his shoulder.

"Looks like it's about to get even brighter in here." Casey pointed at a small compartment above Charlie's head. She tapped on the identical panel above hers, releasing a pair of sunglasses with large bunny ears on each side of the lenses.

"Magnificent." He tapped on his panel and let the glasses fall into his lap, inspecting his own set of ears before donning the shades to help block the light.

They sailed up to the smiling face of a glowing bear and its mouth opened wide, allowing them access to the unknown that lay beyond.

Twenty-Eight

"It's amazing," Casey said, and she was right.

They floated through a brilliant cloud of pink and red hues. There were a few faint thumps as a mist of star dust grazed the sides of the ship. The pink and red cloud faded and was replaced by a myriad of others in dazzling colors.

"This is where I want to die," she whispered, standing up and placing her palm against the window. "It's warm." Her smile drew Charlie from his seat, and he stood beside her.

He put his palm on the window, letting his fingers stretch out just wide enough to touch hers. As their hands met, the cloud of dust lifted from the window and the warmth faded. The cloud arched over the ship, swirling. The multiverse was a wondrous sight to behold now that Charlie didn't have to travel through it by being swallowed by a teddy graham.

The colors of the dust cloud began to change too fast to register, creating a mesmerizing spectacle. It reminded Charlie of the fireworks he had seen so many times as a child. It was awe-inspiring and for a moment, all of life seemed magical.

"I'll die here with you." The cloud slowly dissolved at his words, offering them a view into the swirling vortex. "I suppose that's where we're headed."

"Have you not seen one before? I thought the two of you have been to different universes."

"Apparently you had to request something more elegant than being devoured and forced into a nauseating realm of darkness before being spit out into the world without seeing any of the beauty that lay between."

"You should've asked."

"I really should have."

"He really should take more advantage of the liberties that an interdimensional friend can offer." Frids stepped into the cockpit.

"What's beyond the vortex?" Casey asked, her eyes fixated on the view.

"With the positioning set, it will transport us to the other Earth where the two of you reside."

"Why did we go into the cinnamon one?" The question came out before Charlie even realized he was asking. The tranquility of floating untethered to reality seemed to release the words hanging in the very back of his mind.

"The ones still left above the ship held universes that you were still alive in. If we're going to collect the pieces needed to reconstruct me in your realm, we needed to go elsewhere."

"Where is elsewhere in this world? How do we cover the entire globe to find a small scrap of cardboard?" Casey's question was pointed, but her eyes remained fixed on the last wisps of the cloud passing above the cockpit window.

"We don't. Each memory of a moment leaves a trace in the multiverse: a thought wave that bounces around undisturbed by normal matter, held only by the unseen weight of gravity. It's why random memories pop into your head at the oddest times. These thought waves tend to centralize around you, forming a circle above your head as a falcon would to its falconer. When a thought becomes entangled enough in the gravitational pull of your active brain, it spirals in and delivers a burst of recognition. All of a person's memories and experiences can be accessed through this process."

"If I'm dead, then how would they remain bound to any one place?"

Frids walked up to Casey's panel and scrolled through until he reached the navigational log. "Each memory can be pinpointed with a strong enough search. When its host departs, it remains amongst the strongest living remnant that can carry it accurately."

Charlie thought for a moment, taking a few drags from his vape to aid the process. Outside of people from his youth, no one knew of his unicorn friend. Casey had only come to know about it by sneaking around his room, but she never knew what it was or the significance it played. The only people left to carry that memory would be the people he wished he would never have to see again.

"I don't want to go home." Gone was the wonder and awe from his voice. Charlie no longer cared for the beautiful view, he stared at Frids.

"There isn't another option," Frids said calmly.

"There are more universes. There must be another one in which I don't have to do this."

"Do what?" Casey's trance was broken by the sound of Charlie's voice, and she turned to see him shaking as he gripped the console.

"We need to get Charlie back to his parent's house in this universe. Somewhere in that home is a massive reading of his unicorn. The thought waves don't lie and they are the strongest ones I could pick up on. If we ignore this opportunity, we could be left searching the multiverse for bits and scraps and may never have enough time to complete it before the draw for you to end your life becomes too great to counter."

"But they know I'm dead. They must know I'm dead. You can't just walk into a house as a corporeal ghost and not be unnoticed."

Frids didn't offer a reply. He sat down on his hindquarters and stared up at Charlie, waiting for him to understand.

"They don't know."

"Their thought waves read of a fight between you and them years before where we'll be landing. Even your brothers and sister in this universe are under the belief that you are still alive."

"So even in this universe, they didn't want to talk to me so they didn't have to deal with my issues." Charlie was slipping into the darker recesses of his mind.

"I think you're letting a little bullshit seep into your memory, Charlie." Casey's tone was firm as she put her glasses back into their compartment. "Your brothers and sisters did care for you, but you blamed them for letting your father beat you just as much as you blamed him. They were just kids in an abusive household, too."

Charlie didn't want to acknowledge her point. He had become so accustomed to staring at his memories from a singular view that he had painted everyone in his youth with the same brush. After eliminating contact with his parents, he slowly drifted away from his brothers and sister, too. He had convinced himself that they were old enough to help, strong enough to save him, but never tried. He didn't want to acknowledge that they had been just as scared of what their parents could do when they were angry.

"I highly doubt they have a concern as to whether or not I'm even alive." The words crawled their way out of Charlie's throat. He tried to counter the forces of fear and anger breaking the composure he had sustained since his last breakdown. It had been wonderful to be happy, but it never seemed to last long enough for him to see past the wall of anger he had built around his life.

"Fuck them if they don't, Charlie." Casey stood by

his side, gripping his face in her palms. "We'll be right there with you, and if your parents say a single word filled with spite, I'll slap it back through their teeth."

"If this was what you were looking for, why didn't you just go to this Charlie before he committed suicide?"

"I didn't know what I was looking for until now. This was the answer I needed to find a way to help you. This is the way we save you and the multiverse, Charlie. You have to confront this fear. We need to get that unicorn." Frids sat in the chair behind his console and strapped in. "Now I suggest we all take our seats before we get thrown about on entry."

Charlie and Casey looked out at the vortex encompassing the entire view from the window. Hurriedly, they jumped into their seats and buckled themselves in before the Rockette began hurdling into the spiral oblivion.

Twenty-Nine

The Rockette touched down in Charlie's parent's backyard. He looked out the porthole to take in the view. It was the same as the one in his universe with the same sterile, clean-cut grass. His father had taken to the notion that a man's backyard is his pride and joy. It is to be cared for as if it were a member of the family.

Charlie never understood the concept. A backyard is a patch of grass used for outdoor enjoyment. It is the last remnant of space where people can commune with nature: dig their toes in the grass, watch the squirrels and birds hunt for food, and enjoy the sunshine as it beams life to the world it gave rise to. The notion that a yard should be treated as a still life, unencumbered by the occupants of the household save for a random party to show off its tidiness, was abhorrent to him.

What's the point of saving a piece of nature and attaching it to your dwelling if you're only going to make it look unnatural?

Filing out of the spaceship, Frids tapped his own

chest to open the flap and let the control box fall out. The red button had shrunk in size and now there was a blue button beneath it. As he tapped the blue button, the three watched the ship fold in on itself neatly before shrinking down to the size of a folded dollar bill. It lifted off the ground, flying into a small slot on the side of Frids's box for safekeeping.

"Now we have two options for leaving when we're ready," Frids said, showing the box to Casey. Her eyes were still awestruck from watching her childhood dream, the ship that took them into the wonders of the interdimensional plane, slip into a box no bigger than her hand.

"Why would there be another option than the ship?" she asked.

"There isn't. The other one sucks and we don't need to use it," Charlie said.

"I don't appreciate my work being described in such a facetious manner," Frids said with a huff. It was still hard to take them seriously since his poorly drawn smile could never turn into a frown.

Charlie refrained from replying and focused his attention on the lawn. He hated it. Numerous times he had begged for a swing set or a slide, even just a tee-ball set to run out and play with. There had been a few fleeting moments when he thought they would allow it. But those moments didn't last.

His frustration continued to grow as he stared at the lawn. He was not allowed to play outside of the patio without supervision so as not to damage the manicured lawn his father was so proud of.

"He could've been proud of me." The words slipped out of Charlie's mouth before he could catch them. He clutched his vape and tried to ease his torment with nicotine, but it didn't help.

"Who?" Casey asked, her hand sliding up his back and resting on his shoulder.

"No one important."

Stepping forward, Charlie felt Casey's fingers on his shoulder. Her gentle touch brought him comfort. But now was not the time to fall into wistful thinking of what might be possible in the future with her. There was no sign of any occupants in the household and he wanted to take the opportunity to retrieve his unicorn and leave as fast as possible. No contact with his parents had become the only buffer between him and their tiresome reproaches.

He walked over to the shrub by the right side of the patio, pushing past the stones to find the hide-a-key. Sliding open the bottom of the fake rock, he found it was empty.

"I can always—."

Charlie waved Frids off. He hurled the fake rock at the window on the back door. "No need."

He reached his hand through the broken glass, paying little attention to the sharp edges that grazed his skin, drawing a thin line of blood as he unlatched the bolt lock and turned the knob.

"In and out." Casey stood behind him. "We don't need to be here any longer."

"Agreed."

Charlie left the door open as he walked inside. He could hear Casey's footsteps behind him. Turning, he looked for Frids behind her, but the unicorn wasn't there.

"Down here," the unicorn called as he pushed in front of Charlie. "The last relevant thought wave I could find had the object in the attic."

"How do you know that's right?" Casey spoke for Charlie as well.

"It worked in finding all the Charlies I've visited. My methods have paid off in their locating abilities so far, so I say we continue following their lead." Frids led them up the stairs.

The layout of the house was no different than what he remembered, but the absence of the décor he had grown up with gave him an eerie feeling. "Where are they?"

"I thought you'd be glad your parents weren't home." Casey's tone was gentle but he could hear her concern. "It's better this way. No need for confrontations."

"Not them. My brothers and sister. The photos of us that lined the walls as if to suggest we were a normal family."

"There are no siblings in this universe. It was just you."

"I suppose they hated me even more this way."

"This universe was not kind to you." Frids crested the stairwell, taking a right toward the attic door, staring up at the string that would pull down the stairwell. "Had I known about the unicorn, I may have come here first, but my initial scanning lacked the relevance of its importance and left little probability that you wouldn't have succumbed to the desire to leave life behind."

"Thanks for the vote of confidence."

"It's not a dismissal, Charlie. I just had to take the best opportunities that were left for me."

"I'm not...I'm not mad. I just don't want to be here. I never liked being places where I felt like I wasn't wanted."

Charlie reached up, grabbed hold of the cord, and yanked. The stairs came down and their awkward crawl up into the dark began. It was more cramped than he remembered, but the last time he had stepped into the attic was as a child.

He searched for the light switch but it wasn't there. Then a light flipped on above him. He turned to see Casey's hand on the switch to his left. She smiled and winked, and Charlie couldn't help but smile too. She was beautiful.

"On to the hunt." Frids snapped Charlie's thoughts back to the moment, drawing his eyes away from Casey's into the dusty contents of the attic. "Any ideas where to begin?"

Plastic bins lined the small walkway plywood boards.

Neatly packed and tucked away, he had a sinking feeling that none of them would contain anything of his. "Look for something that is out of place with the rest of this, I suppose."

"How about this?" Casey had crawled down a plank to the very end and held out a busted cardboard box with "Charlie" written on it in black marker.

"That would be it." His heart sank. He had expected to see something of the sort for whatever keepsakes they may have retained. But the realization that his base assumptions were proving right still hurt. Even though, technically, these weren't his parents, he still wished they'd been more fond of him. "Dump it out and let's get on with this."

"Who's up there?"

The disembodied shout rang throughout the attic.

"You two find the unicorn. I'll go deal with this." Charlie recognized the voice. It was his father's, loud and defiant, just as he remembered. He scooted down a plank and got his feet on the first stair. A shiver went down his spine as he headed toward the scolding he was certain he would receive.

"Charlie," Casey called after him. "We'll be right behind you."

Thirty

"I WILL SHOOT YOU!" His father's voice was even louder than he remembered. "I'm not one of those pussies that'll let you walk away with my stuff. You try to take anything and I'll put three rounds in your chest before purring like a kitten when I sleep tonight."

"Good to know you're still sleeping well." Charlie didn't hesitate to make sure his dad knew it was him. His footsteps fell heavily on the stairs as he came down. He felt strangely comfortable with a gun pointed at his head. He had failed to end his life on his own, and the thought of someone else completing the job for him felt strangely appropriate. "Wouldn't want you to spend any time thinking about the shit you spew at other people all night."

Charlie's dad had embraced the new world of social media. In it, he could find ways to shock and offend more people than he could ever meet in person. Charlie sensed he could rightly assume this version of his father acted in the same manner.

Charlie's disdain faded when he saw his mother standing at his father's side. Her hands were slightly trembling. His instinct was to tell her everything was ok and that he wasn't here to cause any harm. He yearned for her to reach out for him and hug him.

"Charlie!" she shouted. Her voice sounded angry, but her eyes were welcoming. "Why didn't you just call and tell us you'd be coming by?"

"Quiet, Miriam," his father said before returning his attention to Charlie. "If you think I won't shoot you for stealing from me and your mother, think again. I'm not one of those pushover parents who let their kids be the boss."

"William!" Charlie was surprised to hear his mother chide their father. For a moment he thought she was coming to his defense. "Just let him leave. He's obviously not taking anything. Don't make this any worse."

"It's good to see you, Mom."

"You shouldn't have broken into our home, Charlie." Her voice sounded colder. He knew her opposition to his father could only last so long. It made him wonder how often she had truly been upset with him, or if she'd just been appeasing his father all those times. She steadied her hands on her purse before she spoke. "You lost the privilege to come in here after your last visit. If you're going to come home, you have to be respectful. We didn't raise you to be this way."

Charlie wondered for a moment what their last visit with his other self had been like. Had his other self decided to confront them, or did they confront his other self for not meeting their standards once again? Either way, it didn't matter. It was too late for that Charlie.

"I'm not here to stay, and I'm not here to apologize. I'm not ready to forgive either of you for the pain you put me through as a child, and even if I was, I doubt that you would even acknowledge it. We're just rummaging through my box of stuff in the attic to get something. Once we have it, we'll be gone."

"What's in this house is mine unless I say otherwise. You want something from that box of trash, you need to pay me for it." His dad kept the gun raised, unwilling to give in to the norm of avoiding lethal force against an unarmed family member. "And I don't care what you think of how I raised you." Charlie could tell his father was frustrated. "What I did, I did to toughen you up for life outside this house. It's not my fault you crumbled like a clump of dirt."

"Beating your child is not the same as raising your child," Charlie said, stepping closer to his parents, ignoring the gun that was pointed at him. "And do you not think that I wanted to make you proud? Do you think that I wasn't desperate for your approval? I tried. I tried my whole life under this roof to make you proud of me, to make you love me. But I never could."

"Charlie," his mother began, "we do—."

"Quiet, Miriam!" his father said, cutting her off. "Sure, I loved you when you were a child. But do you think love outweighs all the shit you put us through?"

"Got it!" Casey's voice rang out from the attic and tumbled down the stairwell.

Before Charlie could speak, his dad pointed the gun above his head and fired. "No one's got anything until I say so!"

"Jesus fucking Christ!" The fear in Casey's voice was evident.

"You want to shoot something so bad, point your gun at me." Charlie heard the words come out of his mouth before he even had time to think them. He went down the remaining steps and stood firm in front of his father. "You've threatened me, bullied me, and beat me my entire life. If you truly want me dead so bad then point your gun at me and pull the trigger, you piece of shit."

Leveling the gun to Charlie's chest, his dad grinned. "You think I'll back down because you finally found an ounce of courage to act like a man? I will level you in an instant, boy. I don't care if I made you. You've been nothing but a disappointing piece of conversation I've had to carry with me at every damn dinner party your mother and I have attended. If I shoot you, at least I can smile when I talk about you next."

"William!" his mother shouted. She reached for the gun, but his father slapped her away.

"Then fucking do it!" Charlie ignored his fear and focused on the anger. He grabbed the barrel of his father's gun and pushed it up against his forehead. "You think I've never had the barrel of a gun against my head?

Do you think the torture you have put me through hasn't pushed me to try and kill myself before? Had I known how to load a gun properly when I was sixteen, neither of you would've had to worry about whether or not I was going to disappoint you anymore.

"So do it. Pull the trigger. Be the man you always claim to be and so proudly announce to everyone you meet. Find the courage to end your son's life and clean up the mess afterward. Because if you think for a second that I care if I live or die after this moment, I don't. I'm content with the notion of not existing anymore. I'm content with never seeing either of you two again, or ever having to worry about hearing your obnoxious self-righteous voice tell me how pathetic I am. Pull the trigger and make everyone's day a little bit brighter, would you, Dad?

"You've always wanted to be the hero in your own story. You've always wanted to protect your house more than you've wanted to protect your family. Well, here's your chance. I'm an intruder, taking something you claim is yours and staring down the barrel of your gun. Be a fucking man and take my life so you can brag to the world about how much of a man you are."

Charlie could see the surprise in his father's eyes. His mother was crying, and Charlie wanted to go to her, to forgive her in hopes that she would forgive him too. He stared into her eyes and she stared into his. Then they heard the stairwell creaking. as Casey started coming down from the attic .

"How about we all take a moment and consider the ramifications of this situation?" Casey said. She was scared. Charlie didn't want to look away from his father, but he had heard that tone before and could tell she was using every ounce of strength to draw closer to him.

"How about you not tell me what to do in my own house?" Charlie's father said, admonishing Casey. "We don't take orders from tattooed junkies who steal from us."

"They're just kids, William! For Christ's sake, just let them go. We'll never see him again at this rate."

"If this is the type of company he insists on keeping, it'll just keep us all the more safer. She was never good enough for this family. And she only made my hopes of Charlie turning his life into something worth being proud of run dry," Charlie's father snarled.

"Well, good to know even this version of you thinks so highly of me." Casey stopped a few steps behind Charlie. "We've got it, Charlie. How about we step back away from the gun and we'll leave with Frids."

"Who's Frids?" his father demanded, trying to aim the gun in her direction.

"You point that gun at me, not her," Charlie said. If someone was going to die for his father's arrogance, it would be him.

"I'm Frids," said a calm little voice. Charlie didn't have to turn around to know the carboard unicorn had stepped out from behind Casey. The fear and bewilderment in his parent's eyes told him what had just happened. "And we're in a bit of an important situation here involving the entirety of the multiverse, so I'm going to have to implore you to put the gun away and leave Charlie unharmed."

"Good to know you care about me not dying this time," Charlie scoffed. And then he blinked. His childhood toy was hanging from a quickly fashioned necklace made of yarn around Frids's neck. It was nearly perfect. His heart pounded as he saw the lines cut and pasted together with care. It was all there, almost. Like Frids, it lacked a tail.

"The last time was unexpected and too quick for me to stop. No need to begrudge the past right now," Frids responded.

"No. I think this is the perfect time to begrudge the past." Charlie was intent on getting out as many demons as he could while he had the courage and opportunity. "Look at me!" he shouted at his father. "You spent so much of my youth belittling me and tearing me down that in countless universes I've killed myself. You've caused me so much pain that I wanted nothing more than to leave life behind and never experience a single moment of existence again. All I wanted was for you to accept me, but that always seemed like it was too much to ask."

"We do love you, Charlie," his mother said. "We just need you to understand what you did was wrong." She was trying to steady herself. Her eyes kept shifting from person to person.

"He'll never admit to what he did wrong, and I'm not going to be insulted by a wretched, ungrateful, and worthless child in my own home," his father said. At last, Charlie had succeeded in getting his father's attention. "I may not have been a great parent, but you weren't a great son either. I wanted a child to pass down my heritage to and all I got was a scrawny wimp with no ambition or skills to do anything more than complain about how hard life was. I wish to God you had never been born."

"Then take the initiative to fix what your God screwed up." Charlie pushed his head against the barrel of the gun, forcing his father's arm to bend. He could feel the cold steel pressing into his forehead and he ached to see the darkness that came from inside the barrel.

But nothing happened. He could see his mother cover her eyes, scared she might have to watch an act of violence she would never be able to forget. And he could see his father's hesitation. Despite the anger and bravado spewing out of his mouth, he hadn't always hated Charlie.

"Let's go," Charlie said to Frids and Casey, turning his head away from the barrel. "I have no need to be in this place for a second longer."

"You ever set foot in this house again and I will end you." His father's voice trembled now. Charlie could hear his regret and shame—he had heard it so often in his own voice after belittling others. It made him sad to realize that he shared in the faults of his father.

"If you ever see me again, it'll be because I want you to. Goodbye, Mom." He saw her place one hand over her mouth. She was holding back her tears and trying not to beg him to stay.

Charlie stepped over the shards of glass in front of the door, swinging it open to set himself free in the open air. Frids stepped out beside him and dropped the flap on his chest, pulling out the cardboard box.

"Ready to leave?" the unicorn asked.

"Yes, please." Casey's voice was trembling, and he could tell she had been crying.

Charlie pressed his hand on the blue button. Being happy or safe meant nothing to him now, but he still wanted it for her.

Thirty-One

Charlie wanted to be alone. When he entered the Rockette and headed for the cockpit, he was not looking forward to being in that tight space with Frids and Casey. As he went up the stairs, a door formed in the wall beside him. Hanging on it was a handwritten sign reading "Keep Out!" It looked like a teenager had written it, and it suited his mood perfectly. He opened the door and closed it firmly behind him.

The confrontation had drained him. He could hear Casey and Frids on the other side of the door, trying to get in. They wanted to talk, to help him open up and release the weight that was dragging him down. But he didn't know what to say.

The solitude felt appropriate but Charlie couldn't hold back his desire to speak. He began to shout at the walls, hoping to release his frustration but it just kept growing. His voice echoed off the walls until he couldn't tell if he was still shouting.

Charlie clasped his hands over his mouth. The

adrenaline that had given him the strength to stand up to his father had yet to leave his system.

His thoughts were getting darker as he drifted into an imagined scenario where his father had actually pulled the trigger. A part of him wished he had. It would have been a succinct ending to a journey he wasn't sure he wanted to remain on.

The fantasy was becoming all too real and his mind was racing. Suicide was calling to him again. It wasn't what he wanted exactly, but if felt like what he deserved. Charlie dropped to his knees with his hands on his head. He wanted to force the thought out of his brain, but it wouldn't budge.

"Why do I have to die?" he whispered.

The silence was broken by a ringing sound. Surprised, he looked around the room and spotted an old-fashioned rotary phone hanging on the wall, its bells clanging. It took him a moment to realize that maybe he should answer it, and he went over and picked up the receiver.

"What?" he said. He expected it to be either Frids or Casey pestering him to come out of the room.

"Hey, kiddo. Thanks for finally answering and using your friendly voice to greet me."

"Megan?" Charlie nearly dropped the receiver when he heard his sister's voice.

"Is it that surprising to find out it's me, calling from my phone? Did you delete my number again so my name wouldn't pop up?" Her question was a little pointed, but her voice was light.

"No, I just... I think I broke my phone and it doesn't show who's calling anymore. I need to get it fixed." Traveling through an interdimensional plane while speaking on a phone made out of construction paper didn't seem like a plausible response, so Charlie hoped she would buy his simpler excuse.

"You suck at lying, Charlie. Always have. But never mind that. You haven't been answering our calls and missed your check in with David last night. He started to freak out and we were about to call the cops to do a safety check on you if you didn't answer. What's going on?"

Charlie struggled to find the words. He couldn't tell her the truth: there was no way she would, or could, believe him. "I'm sorry," he said awkwardly. "Tell him I said I'm sorry. I had a long night at work and must've fallen asleep without checking my voice mail."

"Why do you keep ducking our calls? I understand you had to work last night, but every time we call you seem to have a reason to not want to talk to us. You know we're only doing this because we care about you, right?"

There was a subtle urgency to her voice, and Charlie was having trouble understanding it. He had convinced himself that they were only calling out of a sense of obligation. None of this made any sense.

"No, I know," he said. He shook his head in an effort to break up the fog obscuring his memories.

"Good, because every time we talk you seem to be stuck in the past and angry at us for something that happened when we were kids."

"Sometimes it's hard to get over past transgressions," Charlie said with a bitter tone he didn't intend. It was so hard to remember the good moments in his life when there were so many painful ones. "Sometimes an apology only seems to come forth when people want to forgive themselves instead of having the person they wronged forgive them."

The line went quiet.

"You sound just like Dad."

The words cut him deep.

"How dare you say that. How dare you put me on the same level as him after what he did to me?"

"He didn't just do it to you, Charlie. He did it to all of us. To Mom, to Ben, to David, and to me. I'm sorry we picked on you and teased you when we were growing up. We were stupid kids being mean because we didn't know how to process our own fears and pain." Megan's voice was shaky. "You always do this."

"Mom did it to me, too. She was just as bad as him sometimes."

"She was never perfect, but she was just as scared as we were, and she wanted to keep him from coming after her. She sided with him in hopes that she could calm him down enough so that he wouldn't take out his rage on us."

It was Charlie's turn to fall silent. Conversations with

his siblings always seemed to follow the same trajectory. He would place the blame squarely on them, and they wouldn't accept it. But now he was starting to have doubts. Maybe she was right.

"I don't think we're ever going to agree on this," he said. "Maybe there's just something wrong with me."

"Dammit Charlie," she said in an exasperated voice. "There's nothing wrong with you. You just never want to look past one or two moments of your life, and it's turned you sour. You have to learn to forgive and move forward. Aren't you talking to your therapist about how to do this?"

"I didn't like him," he said. He hadn't intended to tell her that he had stopped therapy, but the words came out faster than he expected.

"You need help. Why do you keep walking away from the help we try to set up for you?"

"I had help!" Charlie's scream rang around the room. "They took him from me. They destroyed him and made me watch. He was the only thing keeping me happy, and they destroyed him."

"Charlie, you're starting to scare me. Try to calm down and tell me what you're talking about. Who's he?"

"I don't need to calm down, and I won't calm down. He was my friend and they ripped him into pieces because they didn't want to feel embarrassed in front of their friends." He was clutching the receiver so tightly it was beginning to crumble. "You have no idea how important he was to me!"

"Charlie, please." He heard her voice crack. The scared sister he remembered from so long ago was returning. But he couldn't stop.

He could hear the anger in his voice. He sounded just like his father. The thought was grotesque and made him queasy but he couldn't control himself. The more he recognized that he was acting like his father, the weaker his grip on reality seemed to become.

"Am I just like him?" he whispered before hanging up the phone and ripping it off the wall. He didn't want to hear the answer out loud. He already knew what it would be, and the though left him crushed.

Thirty-Two

Solitary confinement is not a long-term solution. Gathering his composure, and drawing courage from a puff on his vape, Charlie left the room and headed to the cockpit.

He was sure he had found the answer he had been searching for. He would die and take the demons he'd been given in his youth with him, and it would be ok. Frids found others before him, and he would find plenty more after. Charlie had served his purpose and was owed his release.

The cockpit was engulfed in the high-pitched beats of J-Pop. Casey was dancing, singing along as best as she could despite the language barrier. He had once criticized her for listening to music she couldn't understand. She had informed him that lyrics don't have to be understood to convey emotion. If a song exudes joy, you embrace it.

He leaned against the wall, watching the way her hair swung around her as she danced. Before he set off to kill himself, he had almost called her. He longed to talk to her. But he didn't want to drag her down into his suffering, and so he resisted the urge. She had moved on, and rightly so.

"You seem to be enjoying yourself," Charlie said, working to keep his voice steady as he took a seat next to her in front of the instrument panel. He eyed the nondescript buttons and indecipherable navigation log, amazed all over again at her imagination.

"It's easy when life gives you a chance to understand it properly."

Her words seemed out of place, and Charlie gave her a confused look. "You're going to have to elaborate on that."

"I have a purpose."

"Listening to J-Pop gives you purpose?"

"Big-picture thinking, Charlie. Get out of the literal and delve into the figurative."

"Not helping." Charlie's look of confusion was replaced with a frown. He understood direct lines of communication in speech but got lost in metaphors and allusions.

"This quest—."

"Not a quest." He knew she would glare at him for the interruption, but he felt the word was far too grandiose to be used in this scenario.

"This *attempt* to save the multiverse is the point. This is how you combat the desire for obscurity. The notion that your life is necessary for the continuation of all existence is exhilarating. It's filled with promise."

"I'm glad me having a gun pointed at my head has given you purpose and refreshed your exuberant outlook on life."

"That's not what I said and you know it."

This was his moment. He could drive a final wedge between them and burst her illusions in an instant. "I don't..." His tongue tripped him up. The words were ready to be unleashed to drive her away from him again, freeing him to finish what he needed to do. The tirade he had unleashed on his sister was still burning in his mind. He could access those raw emotions easily if he tried. But he didn't. "I'm sorry."

The hyperactive music filled the silence between them. Casey knew he intended to say something else. Her body tensed up as she prepared herself for it. He hated seeing her like this.

"I'm sorry I said that," he murmured. "Things are just a little rough right now."

Casey turned to the panel and pressed a random assortment of buttons. The music stopped and the cockpit was quiet. "I know that must have hurt," she said. "But those weren't your parents."

"They might not have been mine, but they weren't very different. I heard the same exact words from them in my home. The only thing that was possibly different was that my father would've just used his fists to make his point instead of a gun."

Casey's gaze wandered to the window as a flash of

green light washed over them. "I can't make you happy, Charlie. I've tried. I really have."

"I know, but—."

"Let me finish." Her eyes remained fixed on the window as the green light bent into jagged shapes before easing back into a steady flow. "Your happiness can't come from another person. And your happiness can't be dependent on what happened to you in your past, either. Life's been rough for you, and the universe acted like a complete asshole in the way it formed your mind. But you can shove that shit back in the universe's face. Tell the universe to go fuck itself and finish putting your unicorn together so you can find your portion of peace and contentment."

"It's just a toy." Charlie was getting flustered. Her voice was too gentle, too soothing, and he was starting to lose his grip on his emotions.

"It's more than that and you know it. You poured your heart into that toy and gave yourself an anchor to the world. You don't need me. You don't need Frids. You need the guile and courage you had as a child who created a reason to live."

"I don't think I can," he said. He couldn't really argue with her.

"Bullshit. If you could do it when you were a kid, when you knew nothing about what was affecting you, then you can do it now. Don't shrug off your responsibility in this. Frids and I are here to support you, but you have to put in some effort as well. And I'm going to make sure you do it. That's my purpose, Charlie. To keep you from wimping out and to save the multiverse at the same time."

"I'm only going to disappoint you."

"We always disappoint one another. We always will. Support isn't based on a tally of good and bad moments. I support you because I care about you. Plus, I get to be the savior of the entire multiverse while doing it."

"Wouldn't it make me the savior since the unicorn is mine?"

"Don't be selfish, Charlie. No one likes selfish people."

Charlie chuckled and looked into Casey's eyes. She was kneeling before him, her arms opening to pull him close.

"I see you're doing better," Frids said, interrupting the tender moment. Casey stepped away from Charlie and sat in her seat. "I hope you don't mind that I patched that phone call through to you. I've been keeping tabs on your phone since you said you were under watch after your last attempt."

Charlie paused for a moment. He needed to steel his emotions before he could answer. "I appreciate that. My sister was getting a little worried, plus it's always good to talk to her."

"Is it, now?" Casey's question was pointed. He knew she had overheard too many conversations between him and his siblings and he regretted being so blasé.

"It was short and uneventful. That's what was good." He hoped that would keep her from prying further. But her lips began to move as she narrowed in on his lie. Fortunately, Frids cut her off before she could say anything.

"Ready to talk about what's next?"

Charlie saw the toy unicorn hanging from Frids's neck. The eerie similarities between the two was hard to look away from. "No need to talk. I think we both know where we're going." He leaned back and looked out the window. A glowing ball of fire was growing larger in the distance.

"Good. I was hoping I wouldn't have to pry the information from you."

"I could go for a little prying," Casey said. "Someone want to explain a little so I don't feel like a third wheel on this next expedition?"

"We're going home," Charlie said. "When my parents ripped up my unicorn, I tried to fight back. I failed to keep a hold on it, save for its tail. The memory drifted so far back in my mind that I didn't even recognize the tail anymore, though I could never bring myself to throw it away."

"Where is it?" she asked.

"Somewhere in my apartment."

"Well, damn. That's a pretty easy resolution. I was hoping we could travel throughout the multiverse a little more."

"Maybe we still can." Frids's tone was flat as he

looked at Charlie. "We just have a little bit of business to finish up first. Right, Charlie?"

The unicorn's gaze was unnerving. Frids was staring at him, his scribbled eyes peering past Charlie's façade into his deepest thoughts. He could only try to keep up appearances in hopes that his plan would still work.

"Right," he whispered as the snarling face of a teddy graham grew brighter before them, its mouth opening wide for the ship to pass through.

Thirty-Three

THE ROCKETTE TOUCHED DOWN on Frids's pirate ship to great fanfare. The glowing bears were jubilant, climbing on top of one another to look inside the porthole. The joy on their faces made Charlie realize he had missed the little miscreants. He stuck his hand out the window to greet them, but yanked it back when one bear tried to chomp on it through the glass.

"Let's not antagonize the crew," Frids said, stepping past Charlie to the exit. "Here." He had the toy unicorn in his mouth and offered it to Charlie.

Charlie grabbed it. He felt its rough edges and soft feathery mane.

"I thought it would be a good reminder for you as to what we've been working toward, and what can come from it. We're sitting on the precipice, Charlie. Just give me a little more time and we'll make this right."

Charlie nodded. He didn't have a response. He didn't have any enthusiasm for what was to come.

"Shake out the sourpuss living in your mind," Casey

said, nudging him forward. "It may not feel like it, but this was a success. The next part will even be easier. All we have to do is dig through your dreary apartment for the tail before I can sit down and finish my *Firefly* marathon."

"Feeling a little like Wash, are you?"

"I flew a spaceship, Charlie. I flew a spaceship into a new universe. Of course I feel like Wash."

"I'm not understanding anything you two are saying," Frids said.

"Don't worry," Charlie said. "Most people never know what we're talking about."

As they walked out of the spaceship, they were swarmed by teddy grahams whose mouths were wide open. Charlie and Casey kicked them to avoid being eaten and catapulted into another universe.

"Stop!" Frids shouted, garnering the attention of his crew. "Head below deck and try not to destroy anything or anyone."

The bears looked glum but obeyed the order, dutifully filing off the deck. Charlie looked up at the expanse overhead. Somehow, the universes appeared brighter. Why couldn't he share everyone else's hope for the days ahead? Why did he have to watch the joy he fought so hard to attain slip away and turn into pessimism?

As if on cue, a rough gravitational wave rocked the ship and nearly knocked all three of them down.

"Let's not rejoice in our accomplishment when the multiverse is still falling into disarray." Frids headed for the hatch that would take them back to Charlie's apartment. "What little work we have left to do is still important and needs to be finished."

"Aye, aye, Captain," Casey said, following him.

"Wait," Charlie said, "when did we decide to start calling him captain?"

"This is his ship, and captains respect other captains. Especially one that brought the Rockette to life and made my wildest childhood dream a reality."

"Good to know the bar was set so low to earn your respect," Charlie smirked as Casey shrugged. He didn't really want to argue, but her words got under his skin. Unlike Frids, he had never made any of her dreams come true. He'd wanted to, but he had no idea how to do it.

He took a last look around the ship. The black sails were flapping as the ship rocked up and down on the vast ocean.

"Just a few more steps, Charlie." Casey was waiting for him at the hatch. "Frids already jumped in and I'm not sure I want to be on this boat without him, you know, because of the bears and being eaten and all that kind of stuff."

"Fair enough." Charlie tried to smile and gripped the unicorn tighter in his hand. He felt an intense heat go up his arms and into his brain, where it sparked a rush of endorphins. For a moment, everything seemed brighter. Casey and the ship seemed to glow, casting brilliant hues into the darkness.

"What's wrong?" Casey asked.

"It's nothing. Just trying to see through a different perspective." He moved forward. The creaks and groans of the deck sounded like a song that matched the rhythm of his steps. It was an infectious tune, but he couldn't quite place it.

Ignoring the desire to dance across the deck, Charlie followed Casey through the hatch. The melody ceased as the door of the hatch swung shut behind him. He closed his eyes and let the darkness embrace him. He thought about death. Would this be what it was like? Would the darkness be visible or would all of his senses evaporate?

He had never understood the concept of an afterlife. It always sounded more like a prison sentence than a peaceful reprieve. If you lived in a state of constant joy, wouldn't all sense of meaning and purpose evaporate? And if it was not constant joy—if you could in fact feel pain and sadness in an afterlife—then how was that any different than the life he'd already lived? He'd still be stuck wishing there was some way out.

Before he could come up with a satisfying answer, he tumbled out of his backpack and smashed into his tub. He was beyond tired of this scenario. He'd never enjoyed taking a bath and he'd spent more time in his bathtub in the last few days than he had in the last decade.

"With all the various means of interdimensional travel, why did you choose this one?" Casey said as she fixed her hair in the mirror and helped herself to his deodorant.

"I think your conception of me having a choice in how I reenter our universe to get back to my apartment ignores the fact that this wasn't something I had planned. And why are you using my stuff?"

"This is just one of the small ways you'll be paying me back for helping you out."

"Thank you for informing me of your intent to lay claim to my possessions."

"You're very welcome."

Casey stepped out of the bathroom, leaving Charlie alone in the tub. He sighed at the prospect of staying there any longer, and with a groan he lifted himself out, zipping up the backpack that had managed to find its way back to his apartment. He wanted to ask how, but the thought seemed irrelevant in comparison to everything he had experienced since meeting Frids. There was a lot of noise coming from his bedroom. His first instinct was to tell Frids to shut up, but he couldn't muster the energy to care.

"You're not going to find it by making a mess," he called out.

"This place was already a mess," Frids called back. "You should've gotten here sooner. Now come help us find the tail so we can complete the unicorn."

Charlie was still gripping the unicorn, but its warmth was gone. His heart felt heavy. In the kitchen he set the unicorn down on the counter and grabbed his keys.

"I'm going to go down to my storage locker and get a few boxes," he called out, trying to sound casual. "It might be in one of those."

"Need any help?" Casey said as she poked her head out of the bedroom. "Your arms have always been a little weaker than mine." She winked, her smile stretching wide across her face.

He loved seeing her smile. It was the only thing he wanted to see right now. "Thanks for the words of encouragement, but no. You two keep digging up here. I'll be back in just a few minutes."

"Charlie," Frids said in a dour tone as he stepped out of the bedroom. "It's almost complete. It may not seem like it, but we've come a long way to making your life better since we first met."

Charlie wanted to believe him, but he knew he'd always come back to despair. He had to leave right now. "I'll be right back," he said. He couldn't get the conversation with his sister out of his head, especially his last words to her: *Am I just like him?*

Frids just stared at him. Charlie opened the door of his apartment and walked into the hallway. He took a few calming breaths as he headed for the stairwell. His courage faltered as he pushed the heavy door, prying it away from the latch. With each step down the stairs, he imagined the extraordinary weightlessness he would feel as he stepped off the mountain.

He hurried to his car, worried that Frids may have sensed his intent. The car started and he pulled out of his parking space and headed for the exit. His foot hovered over the brake momentarily, but then he stepped on the gas and drove out.

Thirty-Four

Night had fallen and the parking lot at the trail-head was empty. No one was there to see Charlie banging his head on the steering wheel and cursing at himself.

He had reached a breaking point.

When he got out of the car, he slammed the door behind him. "Fuck!" he screamed. His hands were trembling and his feet were unsteady.

He braced himself against the hood of his car. The warmth from the engine felt good in the cold mountain air. He summoned up his last ounce of courage and began his march up the trail, intent on leaving his car behind for good this time.

Without his heavy backpack and hiking gear, he moved quickly. The cold air bit his skin. Hypothermia was a definite possibility. He needed to keep going.

The beauty and brilliance he experienced on his last trip up the mountain had vanished. He cursed every branch and stump that got in his way and slowed him down. The ground was hard and unforgiving under his feet as he plodded through the snowfall. The winter freeze was not far off.

Charlie didn't stop to take a break as he hurried up the trail. Images of Casey were already tugging at his resolve. She would be angry. She would hate him for giving in and leaving her behind. She would hate herself for not being able to stop him. But she would move on. Everyone moves on eventually.

As the elevation increased, he focused on his breathing. The icy air constricted his lungs, and his leg muscles were beginning to cramp and weaken.

He tilted his head back and looked up as far as he could see. He yearned for answers or assistance. The canopy of trees had thinned out, and he could see the stars above the rocky peak. As he gazed up at the sky, he let out a raspy chuckle as he thought of the glowing teddy grahams. Maybe they would be an audience for his final moments.

"It's nice to have company," he muttered.

He was delirious. The stars began to fall from the sky, and dancing bears lit his path, cheering him on toward his final destination. Charlie shook his head to rid himself of the hallucination, but it was useless. His body was broken and his brain was numb. This wasn't how he wanted to go. It was supposed to be peaceful. It was supposed to be welcoming.

He had the stark realization that his last act of life would be just as painful as the years of suffering before it.

The tree line vanished as he stepped toward the peak. The open expanse of sky greeted him. The moon peeked around the shadow of the sun. Charlie could feel its disapproval.

"What do you know?" he shouted. "You've never even met me. You've never had to do anything but float above the earth. You don't even offer any light—you just reflect it from the sun. Your entire purpose is to be a mirror."

And then he heard a familiar voice, an irritatingly familiar voice.

"Arguing with a planetary mass is an unconventional conversation to have before your death. You're not necessarily wrong in your assessment, but I don't think you're in the right frame of mind to disperse insults on another object floating in space."

Frids stood near the rocky outcrop, staring at Charlie as he had the first time they met. The only difference was Casey. She stood by his side, the unicorn in her hands, its fluffy tail blowing in the wind.

"I didn't ask you to come for a reason," Charlie said defensively. After struggling so hard to reach this moment, he didn't want to feel their piercing glares of disapproval as he jumped.

"You didn't ask me to come the first time either, but here I stand." Frids seemed unphased, as if he had been anticipating this moment.

"I told you, Charlie," Casey said. Her voice was so

weak he could hardly hear it over the wind. "All you had to do was talk to me and I could've helped."

"I didn't come here because I wanted help. I came here because I wanted it to end."

"Don't throw what we've done away." Frids stepped toward Charlie, those scribbled eyes coming into view, that misshapen smile as wide as it always was. "We found a way for you to fight back against this."

"You've found what you wanted. Now go find a different version of me who wants the help you offer."

"No!" Casey shouted. "I'm tired of this. You refuse help from those who've felt the same kind of pain you have. You walk away from the hand that tries to pull you to safety. You aren't doing this to me again."

"This isn't about you. This isn't about anybody but me. I'm not out here because I want to make people feel bad about the way they treated me. I'm here because I can't go on any longer." He stepped closer to the edge.

"You were amazing to me. You were always amazing to me, but that doesn't change anything. It just makes me hate myself even more because I can't be the person you deserve to have. I can't love you more than I hate myself and that hurts. I don't deserve your help. And you don't deserve to have to try and pull me back from the ledge anymore." Loose rocks shifted under Charlie's feet and rolled off the cliff.

"Charlie," Frids said, stepping closer. "I can't stop you from making your own choice. I held you back the first time to offer you a way out. If you've chosen to reject my offer, you're free to do as you wish."

"Take the unicorn." Charlie's voice sounded small. "Find someone who can use it to do what I can't."

"Bullshit!" Casey shouted. Her voice echoed across the valley below them. "If you want to leave, you take this damn thing with you. If you're going to die, then it deserves the same fate."

Before Charlie could respond, Casey was shoving the unicorn into his hands. It was whole again. Tears filled his eyes as he remembered watching his mother tear it to pieces.

He felt a strange sensation in his fingers. The unicorn was warm on his skin. He stared at the emptiness that lay beyond the cliff. Wasn't this the right answer? In a single step he could embrace painlessness. Didn't this make more sense than trying to finding some sort of consolation in the midst of excruciating pain?

It was time to go.

Charlie forced his fear back and leaned forward. His brain sent the signal for his foot to move forward. But it remained planted. It wouldn't move. He looked down, expecting to see Frids gnawing at his pants, but he wasn't there. His brain sent another signal, but his foot wouldn't budge.

"Just let me go!" he shouted. There was some sort of battle going on inside him. The unicorn's warmth increased and spread throughout his body.

"It knows what you want more than you can understand, Charlie," Frids said calmly. The unicorn came over and sat by his side. "If you're going to leave, you're going to have to do what your parents did and tear it apart. Until then, you're going to be stuck here fighting against yourself."

"Fuck you! You have no idea what I'm going through, and you never have."

"You know goddamn well I have, though." Casey stepped forward, standing beside Frids. Her frustration and anger was seeping out in her voice. "You want to die? Fine. Do what Frids said. If you want to step off that cliff, you have to destroy everything you said you wanted because it's all right in front of you. There's no other way. And we won't stop you."

Charlie crumpled to the ground, sobbing. "It's too much. It's just too much."

"You deserve to exist, Charlie!" Casey shouted, her voice echoing around the mountain. "Every version of you left in the multiverse deserves to exist and you hold the key in your hands."

Charlie sat motionless on the ground, the snow soaking into his clothes once again. A battle was raging inside his head—that war he could never seem to control.

"I can't promise to take these feelings away, but I can give you the chance to see a brighter path ahead." Frids pressed his snout beneath Charlie's head, lifting it so they could look directly at each other. "I told you I could help. You've come this far. Why not go a little further?"

"Why not search for the peace that can ease your pain?" Casey pulled Charlie up from the ground and held him. "You don't have to do this alone anymore."

"I missed you so much," he wept. "I never wanted to hurt you." His body continued to fill with the warmth of the unicorn.

Casey cried as she held him tighter. "Then quit crying about it, you asshole."

"Fuck you," Charlie laughed between sobs. "I'm not crying. You're crying."

"How about we all stop crying and go home?" Frids cut in.

"I don't know how to call this world home anymore."

Frids released the control box from his chest with a tap and offered it to both of them. "I wasn't saying you should go back to that apartment. We've got a lot of work to do in keeping this multiverse afloat. You've offered us a chance to right the waves, but we know how to fight back against the draw of the anti-matter now, and there is a multitude of Charlies out there begging for help. Come with me and let's help them."

Casey pressed the button, summoning the Rockette. "You're going to need a little company to keep you safe from yourself out there."

"You'll be leaving your life behind."

"Life is what you define it as, Charlie. I choose to define mine beyond the stars." She let go of him and walked to the open door of her spaceship. "Let's go define yours."

"What if I disappoint you?"

"Charlie," she said. "Stop worrying about disappointing me. It's very disappointing."

He felt a surge of joy as she walked inside the ship.

"We still have a lot of work ahead of us," Frids said. "You're going to need to hold that doll tight as we carry forward."

"It's not a…" The urge to rehash the argument faded. "I don't know how to help."

"To save yourself, you have to confront yourself. You won't be good at it the first few times. But I have a feeling you'll get better at it as we go. I did."

"Sounds like fun." He stepped away from the ledge. Apparently, his feet were listening to his brain again. He walked beside Frids toward the Rockette. "How are we going to get back to your interdimensional plane in this thing? I thought we had to go through my backpack to get there."

"I just did that to get back at you for forcing me to use it when we met. There is a plethora of ways to get there comfortably, I just didn't feel like showing them to you."

"You're going to be an amazing friend to have."

"Yes. Yes, I am." Charlie had forgotten how sarcasm was lost on the unicorn.

Frids stepped inside and Charlie took a breath of cold air, staring at the moon that was staring at him. "Show's over. Go back about your basic business."

The door swung shut behind Charlie as he headed for the cockpit. He could feel the thrusters churning as the mentos dropped into the chamber of diet soda. Liftoff would come before he got to the cockpit. He climbed the stairs slowly as a jolt of propulsion sent them soaring into the sky.

He paused as he passed the door with the "Keep Out" sign, then kept going, joining his friends in the cockpit. He held the unicorn in his hand as he watched the stars fly by. He couldn't stop the smile that worked its way across his face. So this was happiness. He was going to enjoy it while it lasted.

Thirty-Five

DANCING TO THE FRANTIC beats of the song "Sobakasu," Charlie and Casey barely noticed the passing nebulae that were swirling and pulsating along with the music. Charlie had no sense of rhythm and kept bouncing off the control panels, eliciting a constant stream of laughter from his dance partner. But it was worth it. Every clumsy step and awkward bob of his head lifted his spirits higher.

"I fucking love this song!" Casey shouted.

"Me too!" Charlie had asked that it be blasted as loud as possible after he realized that this was the tune he'd been trying to remember on Frids's ship. He had fallen in love with it years ago when Casey first played it for him. "Any idea what she's saying?"

"None at all, and I don't care."

As the guitar riff kicked in, Casey turned up the volume and all the pieces of construction paper started flapping loudly. For a few minutes, there was nothing else in the universe. No pain. No people. Nothing but

Casey and the music.

Charlie reached out for her in an attempt to combine his spastic movements with hers. As their hands joined, they bounced up and down, doing their best to sing along in a language neither could understand. He almost forgot about Frids, the interdimensional being sitting impatiently in the corner.

Walking over, Frids fiddled with the dials and paused the music. The dance party ground to a preemptive halt as Casey glared at him for interrupting their moment.

"Glad to see you two are enjoying yourselves."

"Then why do you look so glum?" she said.

Charlie looked hard at Frids. He struggled to see what she was talking about. The unicorn's expression was the same one he'd become accustomed to.

"Because we've put a brief pause on the collapse of the multiverse, but our solution may not be tenable for every version of Charlie. I've been searching throughout the multiverse and there aren't enough unicorns left to bring everyone back from the brink to have a dance party instead of jumping off the cliff."

"First off," Charlie said, turning to Casey, "how can you tell that Frids looks glum? His expression never changes."

"He's your friend, Charlie. Take the time to get to know him and you'll learn how to read between the lines." Casey turned and pointed. "Literally."

"Fair point." Charlie felt a pang of regret. She was right. In all this time Frids had been trying to save his life, Charlie had never once tried to figure out how the interdimensional being could feel or express emotions. "I'll work on that."

"I would appreciate it." Frids beamed as he took a seat at the control panel. "Now, what's second?"

"Huh?"

"You said 'first off.'" There can't be a 'first off' if there isn't a second thought to follow it."

"Pay attention, Charlie. We just talked about that." Casey thumped him on his head, then leaned over to gently kiss the wound she'd inflicted.

Charlie's heart stopped. He forgot how to breathe. He was frozen like a statue until she whispered in his ear, "Please say something before this gets awkward."

"Right," Charlie said, clearing his throat as he tried to regain his composure. "We don't need to find anything more than remnants of my unicorn."

"And what makes you think that?" Frids swiveled around to question him. "We can't abandon them."

"We won't. We have to see them, as many as we can. If not for them, for me. I have to try. I have to keep working toward helping them or the pull of the residue buried in my brain may get stronger and force me back out to the precipice. We'll find as much as we can and help as many as we can. I don't want to them to die if they don't have to," he said, catching a glimpse of his toy unicorn dangling from a control knob near the ceiling.

"You're asking a lot of yourself considering just a few hours ago you were about to jump to your death,"

Casey said, reaching out to grab his hand.

"Casey, you said that you had found your purpose in helping to save the universe and that freed you to feel the pleasure it brings. I found my purpose, too. If anybody is going to convince me to live, it's going to be me. I have to get other versions of myself to live so I can feel like I have a reason to live."

"The question remains as to how we subdue the anti-matter residue without the unicorns being intact." Frids pointed question cut through the optimism Charlie was finally pouring out.

"What we can find of the other unicorns, I can use to recreate new ones. I lost the ability to rebuild mine when I lost it as a child. That's not the case anymore. I have it now. I have the power now."

"Ok, He-man," Casey snarked. "You have the power."

"Don't be jealous. It doesn't pair well with your brilliance."

"Thank you for hiding an insult with a compliment," she said with a smile.

"You're welcome."

"You're ignoring the rest of the answer," Frids cut in.

Charlie reached his fingers out, taking Casey's hand into his before turning back to Frids. "All I need are scraps to rebuild more unicorns. In this ship, with this unicorn," Charlie pointed to the dangling figure at his side, "I can instill the purpose it had when I was a child. If we break the cycle so many of us go through, it will break the growing draw that you said was tearing so many of us down. Breaking that draw will give us the time we need to convince them to carry on."

"I'm not sure it's going to be that simple, Charlie." Frids stared up at him, but Charlie was starting to recognize the glee hiding behind his somber words.

"None of it will be easy."

Frids spun around in his chair using his hooves to keep going. "You think you can do it?"

"I have no idea. But it's worth trying. Nothing ever comes from not trying."

"I'm in," Casey said, pulling Charlie close and fiddling with the dials. "Back to the dance party!"

As the music returned, Charlie watched Casey fall right back into the rhythm of the beats. He motioned for Frids to follow him out of the cockpit so she could dance in peace. As they moved through the spaceship, Charlie saw enormous posters of anime characters and video game covers springing up on the walls around them. Casey was making this their home, and he loved it. He felt a desire to head home briefly, wanting to grab the Millennium Falcon from his apartment so it could be reassembled in a place where it would be cherished. But that trip home would have to wait.

When they entered Frids's quarters, the glowing multiverse floated all around them. Charlie meandered through the universes, letting them flow effortlessly through his body. The brilliant, swirling specks of light changed colors when Frids tapped them with his horn, animating the lives that Charlie now had the power to affect. He hadn't noticed just how amazing the experience of tip-toeing through the unknown was until now. He wandered through the multiverse until he finally settled in the center of the room. The sum of existence lay before them. The only question was where to begin.

 Somewhere running in the woods or tucked away during the early morning hours at my desk, I indulge in the fanciful images that materialize in my mind and beg to be brought out into the light and written down on the page. Is it magic? Maybe. Is it a good or bad habit that I will never escape? Possibly. Only other writers will know the truth. Thankfully, I have the support of my lovely wife, Jennifer McCaslin, who lets me humor my whims and curiosities throughout the day to make my dream of being an author come true. Keep up to date with all my past, present, and future work at www.minorflock.com. And feel free to follow along on Twitter at @minorflock.